PERILOUS DEPARTURES

Margaret Macpherson

EDITIONS

© 2004, Margaret Macpherson

All rights reserved. No part of this book may be reproduced, for any reason, by any means, without the permission of the publisher.

Cover design by Terry Gallagher/Doowah Design.
Special thanks to Kristen Gislason, Kara Nacci and Molly for cover photos.
Cover photo of Margaret Macpherson by Shelley Chalifoux.

This book was printed on Ancient Forest Friendly paper.
Printed and bound in Canada by AGMV Marquis Imprimeur.

Acknowledgements
"Going Down" was previously published in *Grain*.
The author wishes to acknowledge the support of the Alberta Foundation of the Arts.

We acknowledge the support of The Canada Council for the Arts and the Manitoba Arts Council for our publishing program.

National Library of Canada Cataloguing in Publication

Macpherson, M. A. (Margaret A.), 1959-
        Perilous departures / Margaret Macpherson.

ISBN 0-921833-96-2

        I. Title.

PS8625.L36P47 2004   C813'.6   C2004-901787-X

Signature Editions, P.O. Box 206, RPO Corydon
Winnipeg, Manitoba, R3M 3S7

In memory of my father, N.J. Macpherson,
a lover of life, a consummate storyteller

CONTENTS

CONTENTS

POTTED PALM

Peter is sitting on the heat register again, in his underwear. He's got that look on his face — bliss — as the pumping heat steams up the mirror. He's even made a little tent out of two towels.

"You'd warm up if you got dressed, stupid."

The minty foam in my mouth muffles my insult, so he doesn't quite hear. He's so dumb. And so skinny. I can still see him in the mirror, hunched down so his ribs touch his bony knees, conserving the heat. He's going to be late and then we'll all catch it.

I spit, rinse, spit again then grab the towel off his shoulders and rush out the door, flinging it over the banister before taking the steps, two at a time, downstairs.

"Moooooommmmmmm," his voice still high-pitched, like a girl's. Like mine.

Tim's already in the kitchen when I get down. He looks at me sharply, darts his eyes to the breakfast table and then rolls them way up in his head. Oh, man. Not today. Not again.

The oranges are pre-sliced in quarters. A single slimy section rests on the tray of the high chair like a bad omen. It's already been gummed by Rosa, my baby sister. The bowls of porridge are also out, and that thin scum, so difficult to swallow yet too repulsive to chew, has already formed on top of the steaming creamed curd.

It's one of those mornings. Announcement time. I do a drum roll in my head, and a quick flashback to a few weeks ago.

The last one wasn't too bad. It was about Omar, the kid who writes monthly letters on strange crinkly see-through paper. Once, Peter and I discussed boiling them, the pages of Omar's onion skin letters, when we were playing Lost on the Tundra, but we decided the ink would ruin the onion flavour. We play survival games a lot. They are my favourite type of game. Omar must know about survival. He's our foster child, my age, maybe a bit older. He lives in Chile.

Three weeks ago, breakfast, was the last Father lecture. These are the highlights.

"It's time you children took on more responsibilities." Dramatic pause. "Your Mother and I have decided it would be beneficial if you all contributed to the care of this child." He held up the black and white photograph that usually lived on the fridge behind the crayon drawings and Mom's massive To Do list.

Silence, until Peter piped up. "What'cha mean, Dad?" Then he winced. Tim'd got him a good one under the table.

I heard the dull, connecting thunk. Our dad didn't even notice Pete's eyes going blank and then black. Peter was beaming fire across the table to Tim. Dad went on.

"I want you all to write to him in turn. Once a month." He turned to me when he heard the low groan. "And, Alexis," he added, looking right at me so I sort of held my breath, "I expect you to contribute financially too. All of you. A quarter a week. From your allowance."

Well, like I heard Tim say once, the shit hit the fan then. All of us groaned and Peter started talking about a telescope he was saving for, which was a lie because he was actually saving for a BB gun, and Tim, who is pretty brave, said, "Why should we care about a kid so far away?" and I said, "Yeah, why should we?" And then Rosa tipped over her juice and got yelled at and started to bawl and Mom and Dad got into a big discussion about the whole scheme. That's what Mom kept on saying. *The whole scheme is skewed.*

"The whole scheme is screwed," whispered Tim. And we started to laugh until Dad glared. Mom was really on a roll that morning, what with the skewed scheme. "One child in the village gets supported, and the money creates division. The social fabric is suddenly skewed and the family suffers isolation."

"Money is Power and Power Corrupts," intoned Tim, slurping the pulpy middle from the orange rind. That sure shut Mom up. She looked confused, like she couldn't tell if he was making fun or not, and we would have gotten out of there too, if it hadn't been for Peter, who started moaning about his allowance again.

While our parents debated the nature of charity and responsibility and we sulked about our own injustice and calculated how much our jawbreaker quota would diminish, our school chums whooped by our house on their way to school.

That was the last announcement. Mom and Dad haven't noticed this yet, but if you now look closely at Omar's refrigerator photograph, sheathed in plastic to prevent fingerprints, you will see that he sports a narrow Adolf Hitler mustache of black marker. Tim drew it a couple of weeks ago and because it changes Omar's pinched brown face from sad to angry, I like it better.

Glancing at him, I resolve to write a letter about my all-girl soccer team, the Raving Ravens. Chile once made the semi-finals in the World Cup and I can picture Omar at the game, his pockets filled with my parents' money, the only person from his village who could afford to go. Or maybe that's wrong. After all, he is only twelve.

In my mind I have him watching the match on a large colour TV with his feet on an embroidered hassock. Beyond the window of his lavish hacienda, less fortunate relatives scratch with the chickens for food from the hard Chilean earth. King Omar. This quick fantasy makes him bearable.

The toast is already cold by the time Peter gets to the table. He still looks like goose flesh, all shivery and white. Mom retrieves baby Rosa from the cat dish where she is finishing its breakfast and we jostle to our places. The announcements come only when all are seated and silent and I scowl at both my fidgeting brothers. Let's get it over with. Tim sticks out his tongue just before Father clears his throat and smiles. Uh-oh, worse than I suspected.

"As we approach the Season of Goodwill (he means Christmas) your mother and I have decided we would like to open our home to the less fortunate" (he means someone we don't know and probably would never want to be friends with but should be nice to anyway).

Father's eyes flash around the circle of our inclined faces and his eyes penetrate our glazed eyes. "Peter? Timothy? Alexis? Rosa? What do you think of sharing our Christmas Day celebration with a fellow named Eric who has none of his own people near him?"

This is a rhetorical question and everyone knows enough to stay mute except Rosa, who crows in delight at being at last included in family matters. She's one-and-a-half. I like her because she's a girl, but I sure wish she could do more stuff. She doesn't have a clue about what's really going on. My brothers do. They're both watching our father draw deeply from his coffee cup, questions spilling out of their eye holes like Moose when Jughead tells him Veronica has ditched Reggie. Who is this Eric dude? And where are his own people? It doesn't sound good.

The three-block walk to school is now a mad thundering rush through the darkness. I scramble to keep up with Timothy and Peter scrambles to keep up with me. If the sun comes up, even shimmers on the horizon, before we pass the Hudson Bay store, it means we'll miss the bell. I can't miss any more bells. This will be my third. Three's the limit. After that it's Hinkley's office. Announcement mornings take more time than we allot for our race against the sun, and sealed inside our parkas, hoods like blinders shutting out the cold and each other, we have no time to talk about this Eric.

He is a convict. Father has told us. He is a prisoner. He's coming to our house for Christmas Day, a prisoner from the squat, solid, grey institution near the slag heaps and arsenic pits of the mine. A man named Eric, living in a place we are forbidden to play, will be in our house. A prisoner. Maybe even a murderer.

Madame Hache is conjugating French verbs when the bad feeling really sets in. *Je vais, tu vas, il va, nous allons, vous allez, ils vont.* I think I'm going to throw up.

"Alexis? Are you all right, dear? You're white as a ghost."

In the girls' bathroom I sit on the cool tiled floor amid the clanking pipes and the wet fur smell of winter, and I worry. Eric.

• • •

There are only two seasons in the North. One is the season of light and the other the season of darkness. The season of light is fleeting, maybe ten weeks in all. A strange hazy twilight on each end is called spring and autumn by southerners. In the light we are free. School lets out the same time the snow disappears for good, the same time the sun rises before us and sets long after we are sent to our rooms to sleep.

Once the routine of school ends, Peter, Timothy and I are free to roam in the light for as long as it is there. Our bodies, not our parents, insist we find rest in the season of light. I like going behind the oil tanks, where lichens and moss have carpeted a small indentation in the rocks. That's where I go to refuel. To fill up, so I can go again.

Without the rising and setting sun to guide us, we take on our own rhythms, and our patterns of sleeping and waking become erratic. Our parents let us go in the light, and we are free to roam like feral animals. There are still meals and hours vaguely reserved for being inside, but the rigidity of our household is dissolved by the rare and glorious sun. The air, in that season, is often punctuated with unexplained laughter at odd hours.

I remember once getting up at four in the morning, thirsty, and finding my father kneeling on the kitchen floor in his pajamas. I first thought he was praying, but quickly realized he was transplanting enormous house plants to larger pots.

"They just seemed to call out to me," was his explanation for the hour. "Their roots need more room. Getting bigger is one thing, Lexie, but they have to be stronger too. Winter will be on us before you know it. We must take advantage of the light."

And I drank the water I sought and at 4:00 a.m. knelt beside him on the cold linoleum and sank my hands deep into the soil to form a space for the newly liberated philodendron and the root-bound potted palm while a strange glow, sunrise or sunset or both simultaneously, poured through the window.

Winter's different. From September to May it's dark, a long winter night that makes summer dim and fade until it is barely possible to believe in.

The winter is the time we buy mukluks. Mother takes us. We go down the thin, steep hill that connects us to the Old Town, past the shops, past the two government buildings, down toward the float base and the trading post. The Metis live on the hill mostly, and there's a trailer park. Last time Peter leaned over in the back seat of the car and told me the only white people who lived in the trailer park were white trash. He also said Metis were wannabe white trash. He whispered, so I knew he was saying a bad thing. "It's May-tee, stupid, not Met-ease."

We go every second year for mukluks, always in the winter. We pass Willow Flats where the lake spreads itself thin into a gracious bay. The shacks, painted in mad colours, seem insubstantial, propped up. Timothy says they were here first, but I can't believe it. Our house is so solid, like it's always been there.

• • •

Stella Goodspirit, a grade three kid, comes into the bathroom. She looks at me, flat-eyed and suspicious. "What's wrong with you?" I don't answer.

I watch her go into a stall and see her pants and her underwear puddle at her feet. One of her indoor shoes has a hole at the side and I can see the edge of her sock where her big toe pokes out. Stella pees, flushes and comes out. "You sick or something?"

"Yeah, I guess so." It is the first time we've spoken. I'm sick because a convicted felon is coming over for Christmas. Stella is one of his people. Why doesn't she take him in?

That night I beg my parents to reconsider.

"He's a murderer."

"Alexis, he is not a murderer." My mother looks at me sharply, disturbed by my distress.

"But we don't know that."

"Alexis, listen to me." She crouches down and holds me at arm's length, looking into my eyes. "I don't know Eric. Neither does your father. But the warden knows Eric and the warden would not allow someone...someone...umm, inappropriate out on a day pass. Besides, Alexis," she adds, straightening, dismissing me, "it's Christmas."

I bring my fears to Peter and Timothy, who are reading dog-eared comics in our basement. They prove a bad choice.

"He murdered his wife," says Peter.

"And his kids," adds Timothy. "Eric the Christmas Killer." They are laughing now, mocking me, but underneath I can tell that my brothers are also uneasy about our guest. Timothy's eyes seem outlined in pale blue circles and the tips of Peter's fingers, the skin around his nails, is bright red. They've been chewed raw.

Like me, they know Eric is an intruder. They know he does not belong with us. We sit together in the small, dim rec room while CBC Radio plays jazzed-up versions of "Hark the Herald Angels Sing" and "Silent Night." The tree, two days indoors, is also in the basement. It's next to the furnace, thawing. Its branches are coming down slowly, like a ballerina taking a final bow before curtain. The smell is green, and if I close my eyes, I can almost remember summer.

The boys discuss prison and what it would be like to be locked behind bars. Tim says lots of Indians go to jail. He says the prison is full of them. I wonder how he knows this. Peter says only bad people go to jail. I am afraid he is right.

For small children the night of Christmas Eve is the longest night of the year, and in the North it is doubly so. The night seems to have no end, and it is still pitch dark when Tim and Pete sneak into my room, telling me it is, at last, Christmas morning. The three of us steal downstairs to see what gifts have been laid out at the base of the Boy Scout spruce.

We have each asked for a gun. Three guns, we figure, would make this Eric think twice before pulling any fast stuff. Instead of guns we receive plastic ponies and spinning tops and a family of rag dolls from Guatemala. Pete gets a microscope with a hundred little glass specimen slides and a book on identifying micro-organisms. It's neat, but it's not a gun. I get a doll. Her head, hands and feet are hard plastic. Only her centre is soft. She'll be useless as a weapon. Neither of my parents believes in guns, and self-defense, foremost in our minds, is as foreign to them that Christmas morning as Santa Claus would become to us.

After breakfast Father goes out to get Eric. The roads are slippery, and Peter, Timothy and I are danced into a frenzy, anticipating and dreading their return. "What's got into you three?" Mom asks, swatting the air as if we were dust motes rather than children of flesh and blood. She finally banishes us to the basement in order to run the vacuum across the tinsel-strewn carpet. Down there, where the small windows are covered in snow and the light of Christmas noon penetrates thin and blue, we crouch together in a tight circle, waiting.

When he comes, his face is wide and brown. I don't look at him directly at first. None of us do. We are introduced — Peter, Alexis, Timothy, Rosa — and he repeats each name solemnly. *Peter. Alexis. Timothy.* And then he does something weird. He puts his hand on Rosa's small blonde head, like I've seen priests do. *Rosa.*

"Do you have any children, Eric?" Mom is taking his parka.

He lifts two stumpy fingers and holds them directly in front of his eyes so we see the smile rising behind his hand like a slow summer sun. Some of his teeth are missing, but it doesn't matter. We hang on his intake of air, the chest rising, the eyes crinkling, almost disappearing into the crumple of his brown bag skin, and when he says it shyly, "Two," we laugh as if it is a splendid joke.

In our living room he stands near the centre of the paisley sofa, leaning forward, rocking on the balls of his feet, great hands clasped in front of him. "Thank you," he says of the seat offered. And still standing, looking around the room again, "Thank you."

I see that he is not large, that his hair has been recently cut, and he is not sure he wants to be in this close room with six pale strangers. There is an awful moment when we are all looking at him, but, in that same second, he sits and reaches inside a canvas bag at his feet. He brings out four small packages wrapped in newspaper and tied with twine. He smiles again and holds them on outstretched palms towards Peter and Timothy and me.

Our mother, making appropriate *you shouldn't have* noises, propels me towards him with a firm hand against the small of my back. My brothers too are pushed forward.

"Timothy?" says Eric, dropping the two other packets into his lap. My older brother steps close and is handed his gift.

"Peter?" And he too cautiously accepts the wrapped object.

"Alexis?"

I am next. The gift can't be taken. It must be given.

"Happy Christmas," says Eric, now beaming, and we mumble our thanks and rip at the clumsy paper, ashamed and embarrassed.

Inside my package, coiled like a sleeping snake, is a beaded belt with my name woven in red against a background of black and gold diamonds. Thin green lines run the length of the belt and the lettering is framed in double-sided yellow and blue triangles. Unlike the other letters, the *X* is stitched in black beads like a secret mark on a treasure map, and seeing my name spread out letter by letter against such a brilliant backdrop invests it with new importance. It is magnificent. Timothy and Peter have beaded belts too and Rosa a tiny one with pink buds around her name. But it is mine that is remarkable. It is mine that is perfect.

He made these. I run my fingers over the intricate beadwork. He made these when he didn't even know us. He made them in prison. He formed these patterns in his mind and fit in the letters of our names carefully for this very moment of giving. I look up then, at Eric, and he is watching me.

For the second time he holds up two fingers but this time they are crossed. He is making the *X*. He is saying my name. "Thank you for the belt," I reply. He nods and smiles and his fingers fall together in a loose clasp in his lap.

After that everything is easy. At dinner my parents do most of the talking. They are interested in native rituals, in tribal politics, in the influences of the Christian church on traditional spirituality. Eric speaks to these things slowly, weighing his words carefully. He talks like Peter. He doesn't use any words I don't understand. When he speaks, I get a strange feeling that he is only telling half, that most of what he'd like to tell doesn't have English words. He says a lot even when he's not talking. And he laughs, too, with a low throaty laughter that makes Rosa giggle and the rest of us grin.

I watch him all through supper. I watch him cut his food, put it in his mouth, chew. I watch him listen. Even when he's still, his whole face moves. His eyebrows alone can shout. They're like our Sunday school choir, singing harmony. It's amazing. His cheekbones bend and leap as he listens and nods to my parents' clattering words. I hardly taste the turkey, the cranberry sauce. I can't take my eyes off Eric's face. He is the most exotic person I have ever met and I find myself hoping he will look at me again, ask me a question, or even just smile my way. And, of course, he does.

"Did you get what you wanted for Christmas?" he asks, as Mom clears away the plates and Father goes to his stash of special occasion cigars. Oh, it is a simple question, but my face must betray the complexity of an answer, for Eric doesn't wait long for my reply. "I hope you did," he says. "It is a good time for gifts."

And, remembering the guns, I blush and nod.

• • •

I wore the belt Eric made for me for years and, every Christmas, when he came back, I'd thread it through my belt loops with mounting excitement. He was so cool. Once, I was complaining about having to go out to play after dinner. I wanted to stay, to watch him.

"It's cold and dark, Mom. It's winter."

He looked at me, teasing me with his words. "It's summer in disguise, Alexis. Darkness is light turned inside out."

When Eric got a day pass, he sometimes let Tim and Pete and me hang out with him. He ran a trapline in the winter and knew how to make a fire in the time it took us to decide we were cold. He could identify animals by their tracks, trees by their bark and approaching weather by reading the clouds and listening to a song his ankle sang.

Tim, who's brave, once asked him what prison was like. We were heading back up the hill from the Old Town to home. It was three o'clock and already getting dark. On day passes Eric always had to be back inside by suppertime. I guess he really didn't want to tell us what prison was like. He stopped for a moment, on the hill. He looked at us, bundled in our parkas, waiting to hear. Then he pivoted around and looked back down the hill to the smudge of sun still left in the sky. "Prison can live in your head," he said, "but light lives in your heart." I've never forgotten that.

When Eric got out for good, he went back home for awhile, back to his own people. It was around the same time I had to put an extra hole in the beaded belt. He came back when I was in junior high and took a job with the Public Works department. At first, on weekends and days off, he came to our house. Then he stopped coming.

I still see Eric from time to time, at work on the grader or snowplow, riding shotgun down the road. When our eyes meet he'll grin a big loopy grin and as he flies past we wave at each other in a huge circle that dissects the sky and includes the whole world. That's all. Just that same circular wave every time.

REROUTING THE WIND

After Mother died, I planted a tree in her memory. I chose a Japanese maple, a graceful, ornamental tree with delicate crimson leaves that seemed to flame in the sunlight. I planted that tree the same way we planted Mother, quickly, with relief and regret and minimal ceremony.

I chose this particular tree, I told the clerk at the nursery near our house, because I wanted something brilliant to mark who Mother was and what she meant to me and my brothers and sister. The clerk, who had spoken to Mother on only one occasion, when the furnace quit and her African violets froze, had tears in her eyes as she handed me my receipt.

I suppose I should have chosen a different type of tree if I wanted to truly represent Mother's character. I should have chosen a black spruce, gnarled and hearty, the type of tree that grows in sloughs and scant pockets of earth between bedrock. I should have chosen the type of tree that grows in our and everyone's backyard. But in my mind, black spruce was too common. It wasn't nearly enough for the woman who was my mother.

The Japanese maple, the memorial tree, didn't last the first winter, despite immense efforts on the part of all family members and a good half the staff of Wildwood Nursery. The roots refused nutrients from the soil. The wind stripped the leaves from the branches and today, as I stand at the sink gazing out the window missing my mother, the spindly stick and the lies I contrived to keep her alive mock me.

The transplanted Oriental hybrid was a poor choice to represent the spirit of an iron-minded, oatmeal-touting, moralistic Scot. It was also a fabrication I desperately wanted to believe.

The money for the maple was sent to me by an old friend of the family, Mrs. Alberta Harper. It was an odd gesture, her sending each one of my mother's children one hundred dollars, but I am willing to grant that people, particularly people who are getting on in years, act impulsively and with reasons known only to themselves when they hear of the demise of one of their friends.

Mrs. Harper had been one of Mother's friends years and years ago. She and her husband came into our lives just after the twins were born, about the time Mother finally and reluctantly gave up her job as a public health nurse. For three years, before Mr. Harper died and she ran away with Mrs. MacQuinnie's husband, Mrs. Harper was the local high-school drama teacher in our small northern town. The entire town thought we were lucky to have her, and when she left, lucky to be rid of her. I was never taught by Mrs. Harper, but, judging from the school play, a drawing-room farce with everyone talking in fake English accents, I often felt I was spared unfathomable humiliation.

Mrs. Harper spoke in a clipped British tone. Projecting, she called it. Loud, I called it. She wore bright clothing and kissed everyone she met, twice, once on each cheek. She was always referred to as Mrs. Alberta Harper to distinguish her from the judge's wife, Lillian Harper, she of the tasteful beige and grey. None of us had seen Mrs. Alberta Harper for at least seventeen years, but she likely remembered us as the small children we'd been when our two houses shared a rutted back alley and a propensity for roof rot.

Besides being outrageously flamboyant and impossibly patronizing, Mrs. Harper had an unfortunate set of jowls. Perhaps because the skin hung so loosely on her own face, she had the annoying habit of grabbing our cheeks between thumb and forefinger. Her own fleshy face would become a blurry, jiggling mass as she shook and cooed, shook and cooed.

Because her own parents were long in the grave, and she'd always perceived herself as a motherless babe, I imagine Mrs. Harper considered us orphans after Mother's passing. It mattered not a whit that all of us were well into our twenties at the time. To her, we were still children. The money, sent in the form of cheques in five separate sealed envelopes, was her way of sending orphaned children out into the world with, at very least, a good start and a few bills pinned to the inside of their mittens.

My oldest brother, Doug, who had just fathered the first grandchild and was feeling rather philosophical about the splendid circle of birth, life, death, and rebirth, was mystified and somewhat offended by Mrs. Harper's cheque. I'm not quite sure why. Like my older sister, Doug had not been able to spend much time with Mother in the last days of her life — *the pregnant wife and all* — and I believe he felt Mrs. Harper's gift of money was in some way a small rebuke, a slap on the wrist for being absent at a time when his presence was most required. He put his one hundred dollars to a charitable fund researching the cause of Mother's disease. Later he received a tax receipt through the mail, Mrs. Harper striking his conscience twice.

My older sister, I know, bought a tire for her car. It was a good one, a brand new whitewall with dual treads and all-weather traction, a tire you see on those slick television commercials where you're not sure at first what's being advertised. My sister, whose name is Sylvia but whom we affectionately call Sliv, claimed Mrs. Harper's money was guilt money sent to us to make up for not visiting while Mother was alive or, even more obscure, sent to make up for some slight — real or imagined — in the past.

Sliv didn't have any qualms about spending her guilt money, however, and her practical, unsentimental nature took her down to that tire shop the same day the money arrived. As a tree, she too would have done well in a swamp, although Mrs. Harper's new tire was meant to make sure Sliv didn't end up anywhere near a swamp. Straight-talking, stick-to-the-road Sliv spent her money on exactly what she needed.

My two younger brothers, the twins, didn't have the foggiest notion who Mrs. Harper was when the cheques arrived, conspicuous among the wilting bouquets and gilt-edged sympathy cards. They told me they spent their hundred dollars on getting settled back into university, which I assumed meant cheesy late-night pizzas, parking meters, pinball machines, and beer. Lots of beer.

The twins and I stayed with Mother while she died, back home, in the house where we'd been raised. It was a difficult time. I am glad they spent their money so well.

Because they shared Mother's womb they seemed to share everything, and combining the cash, they could have thrown quite a party, a wild one-night rumpus. Two hundred beers, ten friends, a good way to settle back into university, I figure. But they didn't do that. I suspect the last days with Mother took the party out of them.

I, the middle child, bought a tree. I bought the wrong tree, it's true, but I meant well.

Good intentions not thought out. I can almost hear Mother saying that. It was one of her things, spouting little mottos and adages. *Haste makes waste* when we were trying to hurry through a chore. *Pay the piper* when we had to pee and waited until the last minute. *Spend a dollar to save a dime* when Father returned home after driving all over town to get a good deal on gasoline or some small item of hardware.

She never said these things to be mean. She was not self-righteous or sanctimonious. They were just in her head — quips and quizzels, she called them — issuing from her mouth without thought or restraint. Strangely enough, it was when the quips and quizzels faltered, when they started to trip over her tongue that we knew something was wrong. She began to use words sparingly, so we wouldn't notice the faint slurring that was really the beginning of her rapid and alarming decline.

We always wrote bread-and-butter notes. It was something we were trained to do and to this day, I'm sure most, if not all, of my siblings can't go to someone's home for a meal or stay overnight with an old friend without knocking off a quick thank-you card. I, personally, have a stack of at least ten on hand. It is just something we do, something Mother encouraged and something someone like Mrs. Harper would expect.

Christmas with all seven of us meant opening the gifts painfully slowly, one by one, Mother dutifully recording in a small floral Christmas book the gifts from distant relatives. And each gift had to be treated carefully, as if it only half belonged to us until the thank-you letter was written, stamped and laid on the front hall table to be posted by the next to venture from the warm fragrant fortress that was our home. We would sit, all five of us, at the scarred dining room table on Christmas afternoon, writing the letters together, the more quickly to lay claim to the booty.

So Mrs. Harper, who sent us each one hundred dollars after our mother died, got five thank-you notes. Unfortunately, my note spoke of the tree. I told her how the tree was bright. I told her how Mother was still bright in her eyes — in her mind — when everything else was gone. I told her how the tree spread its limbs and sheltered and how Mother sheltered us long after her arms hung useless, getting caught in the wheels of her chair. I told Mrs. Alberta Harper how the tree was glorious, how it radiated light, brilliant light, like Mother did until she decided she couldn't anymore. I told her it was firmly rooted in my garden and how for generations to come grandchildren and great-grandchildren would gather under its spreading branches and speak of love and life and with that would come, I told her, stories and memories of Mother.

I really laid it on. I told Mrs. Harper exactly what she wanted to hear. I told her everything but the truth. In that letter, the Japanese maple was a twelve-foot-high, flaming, living, triumphant memorial. It was my Mother's spirit tree, and on paper at least, it was very much alive.

My mother died and I planted a tree. The tree died.

When we were young, when Mrs. Harper lived across the alley and we all lived in terror of being cornered, captured, and held to her huge heaving bosom while she quoted Shakespeare in a loud, embarrassing voice, there was a man who used to come to our block selling frozen whitefish. He always came in the dark, in the winter, when he could safely cross the lake on the ice. His name was Jimmy-the-Wind. He was a native fellow, probably middle-aged, but ageless too, and he always traveled alone, door to door, selling fish to us and our neighbours. There seemed to be no pattern to his coming; he would just appear out of the ice fog and arrive on the back porch to do business with Mother. He rarely came across the threshold of our house, although each time Mother would extend the invitation for tea or warmth. From the kitchen window, I would watch him walk away from our house, dragging the fish in a sled behind him, the harness around his hips. He never went to Mrs. Alberta Harper's porch but passed her gate without a look and disappeared into the night.

Jimmy-the-Wind came to our house one evening while we were all piled on the sofa around Father who was reading Kipling aloud beneath the yellow lamp that was the sponge-wet sun of India after the monsoons. Jimmy-the-Wind came to us just before bedtime and for the first time, he was not alone. I detached myself from the potent magic of Father's story and stood in the doorway, in the shadowy archway between kitchen and dining room. There was a child in our kitchen, a small boy, younger than me, younger than the twins even, and this small brown boy whom I had never seen before was sitting on Mother's lap. His brown hair was a smudge against her blouse and his eyes were closed. Jimmy-the-Wind was standing in front of them anxiously moving from one foot to the other, the snow from his mukluks melting and puddling on the floor.

I don't know what happened. I don't know why Jimmy-the-Wind crossed the ice dragging his small sick boy to Mother, but as she held the child in her arms and absently stroked his forehead while speaking in a soft reassuring tone, I wanted to go to Jimmy and tell him that no matter what was wrong with his son, no matter how sick the child was, Jimmy had done the right thing.

Mrs. Harper never had any children of her own. There was a Mr. Harper once, but his name only came up in conversations about dishrags or cat dishes and I imagine him totally emasculated by his large, loud wife. While I was told he died of heart problems shortly before the MacQuinnie scandal, I believe it was humiliation that sent Mr. Harper to that early grave. I have visions of Mrs. Harper grabbing his sad wizened penis between her thumb and forefinger and shaking it, demanding he fulfill his spousal duties.

Her status in our town — a childless teacher who must adore children due simply to the nature of her profession — made Mrs. Harper the obvious person to take Jimmy's boy in for a few weeks while he recuperated. Everyone agreed it would be the perfect solution. Of course, everyone felt sad for Jimmy, but he had other children, surely, and Mrs. Harper would be so good for a boy who hadn't had a good start. Everyone said so. Everyone except Mother.

She would not hear of the boy being taken from his family. She would not concede to the boy coming to stay in town with Mrs. Harper. My quietly moral, strong-willed mother made a fuss. And I mean a real fuss. She went and saw the people in government, arguing against the jurisdictional limits that demanded the boy be brought into town. She went and spoke to the people in her former health unit to demonstrate how jurisdictions were just lines on maps and how easily they could expand to encircle this sick child and his frightened family. Mother even ventured to the social welfare office, where most people wouldn't be caught dead, to speak to them of support and compassion and the social implications of such a wrong-headed move.

While Mrs. Harper went about town talking about how *finally* that la Wind boy, as she called him, would have proper care, Mother followed in her wake, denouncing the plan to move him into town. She even stood up to my father, for he too believed placing the boy with Mrs. Harper would be a good all-round remedy. *Good for whom?* was Mother's rallying cry when the issue of placing Clarence-the-Wind in the care of Mrs. Alberta Harper came up. *Good for whom?*

Mother talked to all the right people in all the right places, but she could not turn the tide of public opinion. The day before Clarence-the-Wind was to be brought into town, my mother put on her parka at first light and, without a word to anyone, including my father, she left our house to walk across the ice to his village.

Her first stop was the pharmacy, where she handed over a prescription she had written herself for the boy's medication. One of our names had been substituted for his, and was silently typed by the disapproving pharmacist beside the instructions on the tiny vial. Then, tucking the precious drug under her arm inside her parka so it would not get cold, Mother walked out onto the white expanse of the lake. For five days in a row my mother walked across our frozen lake to prove her point. It was a twelve-mile return trip, and when she got back, long after dark, icicles had formed on her eyebrows.

Clarence-the-Wind did stay at home and did eventually recover from whatever sickness he had. But for five days in the middle of winter while Mother made her all-day journeys across the ice and back, we were placed in the after-school care of Mrs. Harper.

Eventually the town came around. The new public health nurse agreed to go to the boy; the government agreed to pay the extra cost. Everyone, of course, had heard of Mother's forged prescriptions and her trek to the village across the lake and everyone knew for certain it must be stopped. Mrs. Harper, who came daily to our house to smother us in after-school snacks of a healthful nature and watch over us while we did our homework, called Mother's behaviour undignified and self-important. Spoiled child syndrome, she said, implying that if Mother hadn't caught it from us, we were inevitably going to catch it from her.

My mother died horribly, slowly, like the Japanese maple losing its leaves. First her voice was gone and then her ability to swallow. Next her limbs gave up one by one. In the last few days of her life, movement and communication were limited to her eyes. In those final days, I had a glimpse of what it would be like to be stripped of everything except your soul.

After my mother was gone, I lied to Mrs. Harper. I spent her money on a showy, brilliant tree and, goddammit, I made it grow. I wanted my mother, the memory of my mother, to outshine all the Mrs. Harpers of the world. But in my zeal to celebrate her, I failed to realize she was no flaming maple.

Now I dry my hands and go to the hallway. I put on the gloves I used in the spring to weed the garden and I go out into the yard. It is cold. The wind is from the north and I can feel winter in the air. I go to the naked stalk of the Japanese maple, determined to rip it out of the earth. Some of the branches, tinder dry, break off in my hands, but I grip more firmly and pull it up by the roots. It is not hard to remove, this tree, old and dead. I shake off the clumps of earth clinging to the stunted roots and I carry the tree down to the burn heap at the bottom of the yard. As I heave its awkward weight onto the top of the garden refuse I think of Mother and, turning to go back inside, I am struck by the sound of wind singing through the branches of black spruce.

TRIP OF A LIFETIME

They are in California, Disneyland almost. They have taken a motel just on the outskirts of the Gates, so it is moderately cheaper, being as there are seven of them. The monorail is within walking distance, and every second night when Gail has to sleep on the carpeted floor of the motel room so one of her brothers can have one of the two double beds, she can feel the vibrations of the train as it swooshes by their window.

She doesn't mind having every second night on the floor. Those are the nights she's allowed root beer with her dinner in the motel restaurant, Captain Long John's. The children in beds have to have milk. This is their mother's rule and their mother is the boss because their father isn't with them. There was supposed to be another boss, their

cousin June, a long-legged, shy teenager. She was coming to
help with the children. Or that was the idea. Now June has
pink eye and has to stay in the hotel room. She spends most
of the day watching television through puffy swollen eyes.
She has her own bed, too. Something about segregating the
sheets. It doesn't seem fair.

So now Gail has to be in charge of Donk, whose real
name is Daniel. Her older brother Joey is in charge of Suz,
who is the smallest, and then there is Clare, her very oldest
sister, with her mouth painted cherry red and mean, who
thinks she's in charge of the whole world. They are in
Disneyland because their father is in summer school. Mother
has taken them away, on the "trip of a lifetime," so their dad
can study.

Gail wonders if this is a good thing for her mother.
She thinks her fair, red-headed mother looks like an
overcooked carrot, wilted and mushy. The constant paved
heat and the huge surreal costumed cartoon characters who
walk the promenade and try to engulf small children in their
stick arms make her mother uncomfortable, Gail can tell.
They are in America. Minnie and Mickey are Americans
dressed up in big mouse suits. Minnie might have a gun in
her red purse. You have to be careful around Americans,
cautions her mom. Americans are not like us.

They are from Canada. Joey and Suz and Donk chant
it; the song they all learned last year at confederation: "*Can-
naa-da, We love thee, Now we are twenty million, Can-naa-
da.*" Gail never sings it. It's not the 1967 part that bothers
her, that's good, that means the country has lasted a hundred
years, one hundred years without getting blown to bits by
the gun-toting Americans or, worse yet, the Russians with
their bombs. She crosses her fingers, hoping but not really
believing that Canada will last another one hundred years.

She's almost certain it can't last. Not with twenty million people. That's the part of the confederation song she never sings. It makes her feel sick and small to be one of twenty million. It makes her disappear.

So does Disneyland. She likes it, but in a way, it remains suspect. She wishes she could be like Suz, who runs around like crazy and looks at everything and laughs. Or even Donk and Joey, who whoop and gallop through Fantasyland and past Tinkerbell's castle like it's normal. They want to go on all the rides and eat masses of pink cotton candy and spun toffee on a stick until they collapse at the end of the day, happy and ready to start over.

Clare? Well, who knows about Clare? She acts like she's too old for it, but you can tell she likes the bright colours and the rides and the way the boys look at her long brown legs in cut-offs. Clare is like Mother, minus the stress and the love. She doesn't talk to Gail much. But a few minutes ago she asked her to pretty please go get cotton balls from the hotel room, from the little black cosmetic bag in her suitcase, because June was going to do her toenails. Gail could tell she was being fake, especially when she said *cosmetic* like she was a grown-up, trying to impress pink piggy-eyed June who wiggled in her two-piece in case someone around the pool was watching.

But Gail got the cotton balls anyway and hung around watching until they told her to buzz off. Now she's with Joey and Donk at the shallow end of the turquoise pool. Suz is lying down with Mother because she had a fit at Captain Long John's last night when the drinks came and the root beers weren't for her. Suz can be such a baby, especially when she's tired.

They are on day four of their six-day "trip of a lifetime" tour. In two days they will fly back to Canada and then take

the train to Edmonton. Thinking about home makes Gail
wish it would come sooner. She'd like to see their house again
and make a fort under the weeping willow in their front
yard. It's so quiet and private there, with the branches a cool
canopy of green. Not like this, where the colours scream their
garish uncommon names in the shimmering Californian heat.

Donk and Joey are getting out of the pool, their little
bodies streaming. Their trunks hang low, hugging the angular
contours of wet boy. Gail looks once and then quickly away.
She feels her face flush hot. If she were a boy she could be
with them, sputtering and clowning and shooting water from
her mouth in amazing arcs. Or if she were older, painting
Ruby Blush on her own stumpy toes. She imagines Suz, damp
and sleeping, enveloped in the warm cave her mother has
formed with her own long body.

Donk pads past on the steaming pool cement. He's
going to the deep end. He's going to ask Clare for a Popsicle.
Gail knows he won't get one. Popsicles, here in Disneyland,
are a treat between 3:30 and 4:00, the same way cookies and
milk are an after-school treat at home, something to tide
them over. They only go inside the Gates in the mornings
when the lines aren't too long. The hot afternoons are spent
at the motel, mostly in the courtyard, mostly here, at the
pool, while Mother sleeps. It's better that way, cheaper and
less frantic.

Gail eases into the pool. The water is cool and feels good
on her skin, which is the same pink as her cousin June's eyes.
Her bathing suit is from last year and it's too small. Gail's straps
dig into her shoulders, the crotch tugs up. Still, it's better here in
the water than on the edge where everyone can see her. In the
pool she's light and can imagine herself gliding through the water,
graceful and slender like the ladies on the television commercials
for healthy breakfast cereal. Gail can't swim. At home, she's been

too self-conscious about wearing a bathing suit in public. And it never really got hot. Not like this.

Joey is watching her. He's almost thirteen but even though he's older, he's still way smaller than she is. He's skinny. She's not. *Mother,* her dad jokes, *our Gail has a hollow leg. Feed her up, feed her up.* And they do. If you're large enough you can't vanish.

She bobs in the pool, loving the weightlessness and the coolness. Joey smiles encouragement from the edge. Every time she bobs up, she goes a little bit farther out. The pool bottom slants down. She's too deep. She's over her head. She jumps, getting her face out, grabbing enough air to call to Joey. He nods. "Good," he calls. "Good."

She goes under again and it takes longer for her feet to touch. When they do, she pushes up with all her might. Joey is there again through the panicked blur, waving and smiling. Down again and farther out.

Now Gail can just get high enough to grab a little air. When she opens her mouth to call out, water flows down her throat. But she can't cough or call. Joey is there, way above her, losing interest. He's looking for a Popsicle. Does she hear Donk crying? No, it's water rushing into her body, filling her up, making her so heavy she just lets go and sinks into the muted blue.

Strong hands around her waist thrust her body upwards and she cracks the surface like a shot. It's too bright and dizzying, all of a sudden. The tiles of the pool scrape and grate, and someone is pushing on her chest until the chlorinated water works its way up her throat to dribble out in sputters and coughs. She's saved. Gail is saved. She opens her eyes to see a stranger above her, a girl, maybe twenty-one, certainly older than Clare, maybe even older than cousin June. She is slick and smooth, as one just born, still in the transparent state of streaming wet. Droplets of water form and drip from her face onto Gail's face like hot tears. She is smiling. Her teeth are big and white and even. It is the most beautiful smile Gail has ever seen.

"You're okay now."

And because it is a statement, not a question that needs an answer, Gail starts to weep. Suddenly everyone is there, gathered around her like a hug. Her mother, looking disheveled and worried, is crouching, helping her sit up. Clare and June, like cockatiels come home to roost, with their ridiculous bright talons spread and separated, are fluttering and flapping around Gail, alternately cooing and cawing alarm and sympathy. Joey is there, looking like he did something wrong, and blank Donk, not sure what's going on but not wanting to miss the action. Even Suz can be heard, in the background, wailing.

Her family is in clear and perfect focus. But something is missing. Gail knows there should be one more person in the circle but the woman who saved her has disappeared. The puddled water poolside still glares at the sun. The limp palm fronds still waver in the heat. Her family huddles, close, but Gail can only see one thing in her head. It is a dive, a running dive, a perfectly executed running dive, performed with no forethought, no show, no hope of honour. She sees a flash of white, something hovering and then descending. In her mind, Gail recreates that powerful force moving down upon her and quickening her slack body to hasten their joint ascension into the riotous colours of the world.

NO LONGER THE NARROW WAY

The summer the Soviet space satellite fell from the sky was the same summer she shortened her name to Cyn. The events of that season are as intertwined and inseparable as the Siamese twins peering back at her with implacable disdain from page 184 of the *Guinness Book of World Records*.

Again and again with a morbid fascination, Cynthia went to that photograph, inexplicably drawn to the brothers joined at the waist. Two heads and two sets of eyes stared. From the brothers' shoulders four functional arms extended, but below the armpits the men morphed into one being. They had only one torso — one body, really — yet from below the waist, four legs scissored. The eight limbs protruding from the body made Cynthia think of an exotic spider, repulsive but fascinating. The twins shared a blood system and internal abdominal organs, and, according to the text, they were married to two different women. It left Cynthia reeling.

In 1978 Cynthia had a summer job, her first out of high school. It was a great job, a government job, an outdoors job with lots of fresh air, sunshine and good money to boot. She was hired as a surveyor's assistant. She was the only female on the team — this was also good, although she wouldn't know that until later — and their project, or at least what she could understand of their job, was to straighten a road.

Long before there were cars, or white people, for that matter, there had been a trail that went from town through the bush to a deepwater lake. It was a fourteen-kilometre walking path, traveled well enough that over time it evolved into a cart track, and then a skidoo trail, before finally becoming a narrow, washboard road. As the town grew, the road became more widely used and tar and gravel were laid on the roadbed. Picnickers and weekend partiers drove to the lake to get away. Cabins were erected. A small store was established, selling bait, Coca-Cola and mosquito coils.

The serpentine road, officially named Ingraham Trail, was treacherous, however, and when a family of tourists in a fast car immolated themselves on an outcropping of rock, the town decided the unruly, organic road needed to be tamed, straightened and legitimized. By the time it became apparent Cynthia was to be hired — token female on a long list of applicants — she'd recreated herself. "They call me Cyn," she said to her senior supervisor, Harley, who was cute in a denim jacket, smokes-rolled-up-in-the-shoulder kind of way. She cast her eyes downward, and felt her cheeks heat up by the lie.

A flicker of interest passed across Harley's handsome face. She saw the smirk, the eyes smiling, taking her in; "Sin," he repeated. The tip of his tongue poked out past his teeth "Okay, Cyn it is. We meet every morning at 7:30 a.m. Bring a lunch."

That summer surveying job was punctuated by four major events — five, if you include the arrival of the Soviet space satellite. The surveyors hired on the Ingraham Trail project made way for the blasters, the large rough men who would determine how much bedrock needed to be removed. They would mark the rocks for drilling, preparing the place where long cores of stone were drawn out, creating a hole the exact circumference of a single stick of dynamite. Cynthia loved that part, watching the shaft of dynamite slip down the narrow hole and then waiting, waiting for the explosion.

Four times that summer, in the pre-dawn hours, Cynthia gripped a fluorescent road sign that said STOP: BLASTING IN PROGRESS and watched bedrock implode, bits of Precambrian Shield fly into the air, the result of her team's mighty and earth-shaking efforts to make straight the way. Between the blasts were countless tedious hours of standing alone in the bleaching sun or pelting rain in a blackfly swamp holding a stupid pole while a man, hundreds of metres away, squinted though a tiny instrument and waved his arms madly. *What was that signal supposed to mean?*

"Cyn," they'd call. "Pound stakes." Or, "Cyn, flag the bush at forty-five degrees," and she'd smile her secret girl smile, feeling the power of her new name on their lips, and trot off to do what she was told. Cynthia grew stronger and browner and her hair bleached out in the sun. She kept it up, ponytail poking through the back of the Blue Jays ball cap she'd lifted from her brother's collection, but at the end of the day she'd shuck off the cap and let her hair fall to her shoulders, reminding everyone she was not only female but *the* female.

The road works summer of 1978 she learned to play cribbage at lunch hour, *fifteen-two, fifteen-four and a pair is six*. She learned that Harley, the big boss, would choose her as his assistant on cloudy days when they were stuck in the truck for long periods of time but on fair days he'd always choose one of the boy assistants, who were better in math and had an innate appreciation of heavy-duty equipment.

Cynthia learned that wearing a certain pair of cut-offs and a tank top always made the grader or cat operators gear down, and that mosquito bites didn't go all red and blotchy unless you scratched them. While she never really understood the calculation of angles and the trigonometry involved in road building, she spent hours watching ducks build nests on the edge of the sloughs. She saw the male duck preen, chartreuse neck proud and strong, while the dowdy female worked in the weeds building for the future.

"If we were birds we could just fly to wherever we wanted to go," she said to Harley once, about halfway through the summer, as he was bent over his calculator and his field book. "We wouldn't need to do this job. Ducks always fly in straight lines."

"You got a brain like a bird, kid," he replied, barely looking up. "Did you know they now breed birds with breasts so big they can't fly? Makes for good eating. Small brains, big tits, nice combo, except when you're trying to get some work done." And she blushed and shrank back into the cab of the truck, pushing her shoulders up to stop him looking.

At home, almost every night before bed, she'd look at that photo of the Siamese twins and imagine being the one that had to turn a blind eye. Was he able to shut down his sensory systems when his brother made love to his wife or did he get the pleasure too? How could he help it? And why was she thinking about it all the time?

And then Cynthia's thoughts would shift over to Harley and being in the truck with him on cloudy days or, even better, when it rained. How the windows would fog up with their breathing and how sometimes he would turn on the radio low and talk to her about the difficulty of plotting spiral curves or determining position by celestial navigation as they waited out the rain. She thought about what she wanted and what she didn't want until it would meld into a single mass in her mind and she'd sleep restlessly, bothered by some piece of information that wasn't quite there.

It was worse on Sundays. On Sundays when Pastor Brad denounced the fickle nature of man and pleaded with his flock not to stray, not to take the broad highway of certain destruction, Cynthia would conjure those Siamese twins and in her mind trace her way up the multiple legs to the organs that lay at the very middle of their shared self. Sometimes, if the sermon was long or tedious, she would imagine one of the brothers with a face like Harley's, but for the life of her she couldn't imagine his other twin half.

The satellite fell three days after their last blast, a final unexpected crescendo at the end of a hot, wet summer.

The Soviet space satellite was supposed to burn up when it re-entered the earth's atmosphere. At least, that's what Cynthia had heard on the news the night before, while packing her lunch. It hadn't all disintegrated, however, and a piece of it was lying in the bush just past their last blast site, a few kilometres up from where a centre line of fluorescent-tipped stakes marched straight into a swamp.

It was Harley who took her to the site near the river. "Don't get out of the truck," he said as they pulled off the road and parked. "It's over there. It might be radioactive. If anyone comes, make sure they don't go further than this."

"But I thought I wasn't supposed to get out of the truck."

"You can't go past it, Cyn. Don't go exploring. Just sit here. This is serious." He looked at his watch, frowned, and started to gather his gear. "Trevor's picking me up in his truck. We're going to the job site. I'll come back at noon. There's a guy flying out from Ottawa right now, some sort of nuclear research guy. Don't worry. Just don't let anyone go beyond the truck. You're safe here, but no closer. You understand?" And then, with Trevor's truck skidding into the gravel and spitting back dust, he left. She was on guard.

At first it was great, like a day off, guarding something you couldn't even see. But then it got boring. What was out there, anyway? How did it look? What would it do to her? What *could* it do to her?

Squinting through the windshield Cynthia could only see scrub trees, roots and rocks, and the poor sandy shale ground where hardly anything grew. Would the satellite emit an eerie green glow? Would it cause her babies to be born with two heads, the Siamese twins recreated? Or would its energy melt her, the same way the Japanese people had been melted when the Americans dropped their nuclear bombs on Hiroshima and Nagasaki?

But no, this wasn't a bomb. Dynamite was a mini-bomb, a kind of bombette, and she wasn't afraid of blasting at all. In fact she liked it. Blowing up the bedrock was the best part of her job. After the blasting, Harley, all tease and smile, would call her to ride back to town with him and they'd share a cigarette. He'd flick the butt out the window and drape his arm across the bench seat so she could almost feel his fingertips.

This thing wasn't a bomb. No, this was a satellite, maybe even a Russian spy satellite. Weren't the Soviets Red Communists who brainwashed people into believing religion was bad for you? Maybe the satellite was one of their broadcast systems and if she got out of the truck and into its range she'd suddenly hate God, and all the rules that told her what she could and couldn't do would fall away.

By midday Harley still hadn't come. Cynthia was hungry and she had to pee. There was no choice but to get out of the truck.

The wind was cool and felt so good after the stuffy interior of the cab. Cynthia looked briefly in the direction of the alleged satellite and then ducked into the bushes adjacent to the rear wheel. Because she was in mid-stream when she heard the vehicle, she crouched lower instead of standing up.

Through the willows and the spruce she could tell it wasn't Harley. It wasn't anyone from the surveying team. A strange man got out of a silver-blue rental car. He had red hair and freckles, a nice build, although Cynthia couldn't quite see his face. He was wearing a pair of jeans and a white T-shirt, brilliant like something off a laundry commercial. She didn't move a muscle. He mustn't look her way. Carrying a small hand-held rod with some sort of box attached, the man approached her truck, peered in and then looked around. She didn't breathe.

He frowned and then turned some dials on the box and started walking in the direction of the Soviet space satellite. When she was sure he was gone, she stood, tugged up her shorts and walked over to the truck. Harley hadn't come back, as he'd promised. He probably wouldn't come back now until the end of the work day. He didn't really care very much about her, anyway.

She could see the stranger's footprints in the sandy soil, heading straight towards the forbidden satellite. It couldn't be that bad, she thought, glancing first at herself in the driver's side mirror. She straightened her back and bit her lip. It was time to find out. Time to get the missing information to figure out the final equation. She couldn't sit immobile and unknowing forever. Whatever the poison, whatever the pleasure, she was ready.

Taking a deep breath, Cynthia followed the imprints of the unknown spaceman towards the Soviet space satellite. He was crouched down, his back to her, when she crested the bank above the river. Cynthia noticed he was wearing a sort of oversized white lab coat now and his hands were sheathed in large aluminum gloves. She could see his hands moving, light and nimble, by the flashing reflection of the sun. It was time. She stepped forward just as the shelf of sand she was standing on gave way. She grabbed at some scraggly wild rose bushes to slow her descent towards the rocky beach where the scientist was suddenly now on his feet. He was shielding the thing in front of him, placing himself squarely between Cynthia and the satellite.

"What the heck..." he cried, abruptly pushing back a strange shield that looked like a welder's mask from his face. There was a strange silence after the cessation of movement. Birdsong could be heard and wind on the water. The man looked at Cynthia and Cynthia looked at the man. His body, in what she guessed was an asbestos suit, was brilliantly, radiantly white and his hair under the crown of his dark mask was the colour of fire.

"My hands are bleeding." It was the only thing she could think of to say.

He came toward her then and looked into her upturned palms. The thorny branches had sliced the fleshy part of her thumb and below the first finger joints, on both palms, miniscule droplets of blood were forming where the thorns had pierced.

The scientist pulled off his huge metallic gloves and held both her hands in his. He whistled low. "Yup, you've done a number on those." He looked up then, his eyes meeting hers, still holding her hands. "What are you doing here?"

Cynthia watched the blue eyes dance between suspicion, concern and amusement. It was suddenly impossible to lie. "I heard it was bad," she said, gesturing to the object down the beach. "But I wanted to find out for myself. I was supposed to be keeping people away, but nobody told me from what." It sounded so young and so impossibly lame Cynthia bowed her head, feeling the tears threaten.

A hand was suddenly at her side, propelling her up the beach away from whatever the thing might be, away from whatever it might emit. The hand on her waist felt light and meaningless, as well as heavy and purposeful. It was stinging and healing her at the same time.

The young scientist spoke gently, as though he had known her for a long time. "We can talk about it," he said, "but first we'll go to my car and see about those hands." He looked back down the beach and seemed to speak to the river, the wind in the rustling trees and the twisted lump of metal, now small and insignificant. "Things are pretty much under control here. It could have been a lot worse. A lot worse. Everything will be fine."

As she picked her way back up the crumbling slope, Cynthia could feel the sun warm on her back. Somehow she knew with a new certainty the scientist of the Soviet space satellite was right.

THE CHINESE

Squatting on Main Street between Edna's Fashion Fabrics and the Imperial Bank of Canada, the dun-coloured building was a fixture in our small, dry town, a place that had always been there. Simply called The Chinese, it defined something central, marking the town itself off from the endless sea of fields.

It was not an impressive building like the bank, which boasted stone pillars and had the added import of Roman numerals etched on its scowling edifice, but for most, particularly for those of us who lived on farms, the Chinese café held a potent allure. It was a plain building, but it possessed a forbidden, seductive charm, rather like the Strangers we were warned about, the faceless men who offered us candy or claimed to have a puppy we'd surely want to see.

It's difficult to explain the compelling nature of The Chinese, but ever since I can remember, it tempted, calling, indeed luring us into its dark, crimson interior.

The plants growing in the steaming windows were the first indication that something mysterious and exciting loomed behind the double glass doors. These were unlike any other plants I'd seen. A rampant jungle of fat rubbery leaves on gnarled trunks competed for space with hairy green tendrils dripping brilliant red flowers like tiny spots of blood. There were spiky things too. Spiky yellowing shafts emerging from plastic pots defied the very nature of planthood. These were wild, foreign things, mocking the sterile pots of limp African violets carefully nurtured by our mothers in the gauzy half-light of unused living rooms.

The Chinese restaurant wasn't exactly forbidden by my parents but it wasn't encouraged. On regular weekend trips into town, lunch, or occasionally a cup of tea, was taken at the Park Hotel or, more often, at the lunch counter in Kresges. There, my younger brothers and I would turn idly on the bum-worn stools, attempting to filter out the odour of stale cigarettes and cooking grease to inhale the impossibly sweet smell of all things store-bought.

Kresges was good in a familiar and non-threatening way. Rather like a visit to our Aunt Helen, who never failed to give us each one licorice allsort, Kresges was a predictable treat. New underwear at the beginning of each school year we would get routinely from our department store; adventure, excitement, never.

The year I started high school was the year the Chinese café came to glow like a beacon of personal autonomy. It signified my independence. It called *my* name.

Seven of us became bus kids that thrilling September we started at Central Collegiate. Seven of us country kids weaned of neighbourhood elementary were starting school in town. Few things in my adult life have matched the largeness of that event. The yellow school bus, scheduled to pick me up at the top of our lane every morning, was the hallmark of liberty. Little did it matter that Eugene and Harvey Evans, the pimply brothers from the neighbouring farm, were also on my bus, or that Greta Kindersley, whom I had known forever and never liked, patted the seat next to hers in some desperate attempt at allegiance. What mattered was that I was finally on my way to bigger and better things. Overdressed and masking my nervousness in a casual and awkward indifference, I boarded the bus and purposely sat with the only girl I did not know.

She was huge. Big as a house, big as a barn, big as anybody I'd ever seen. Strangely, her face was tiny and perfect, an island oasis in a sea of undulating flab. The dress she wore was red with small white flowers printed on it. The fabric looked like awning material, all stiff and heavy. If she was that fat, she had to be lonely.

"Hi," I said. "I'm Hanna without the H."

She didn't say anything at first, just squeezed up against the window trying to make herself smaller, to make room for me.

"That would be Anna." She said it so softly I almost didn't hear.

"What?"

"Hanna, without the H."

I laughed then, probably more because I was nervous about starting school than anything else, but the laughter seemed to help and after the colour that rose in her face subsided, she smiled too.

Her name was Vivian Rumple. Her family was from a
dirt-poor scrub farm north of ours. She had done her
elementary school at home. Her dad taught her, she said,
but he didn't understand the math anymore and so she'd had
to come to town.

Vivian didn't tell me all this at once. It took weeks to
find out. She wasn't what you'd call a talker. Not at first.
Every morning and every afternoon we'd ride the bus together
and slowly I got to know her. Our friendship — if that's
what it was — was limited to the hour before and after school.
During school, as if by some pre-arranged agreement, we
never spoke. I'd see Viv, more an environment than a human
being, coming down the hallway, impossible to miss, and
we'd pass each other in the hall with just the slightest glance.
She'd smile. I wouldn't. It was a wordless pact that was never
broken.

I might have acknowledged her if she weren't so fat,
but I knew one word to Vivian Rumple would disqualify me
immediately from the group of girls whose company I
coveted. They were the popular ones, the trend-setters, the
girls who knew secrets but never, never told. They giggled,
they liked certain boys, they were given special duties by the
teachers — dust out the chalk erasers, take the attendance
sheets to the office, speak at the assemblies. These girls had
power. If I was remotely close to being accepted, Vivian didn't
have a chance. Not a hope in hell.

It was after Halloween when we first felt the draw of
The Chinese.

It was owned by a family of Marks, who had been in
our town since the railway went through. First the father
had come, setting up shop in a tiny building off Station Street,
halfway between the slaughterhouse and the Park Hotel. The
wife had come a few years later and later still, her parents,

wizened and foreign, jabbering in their unknown tongue. They all lived in that first restaurant, behind the kitchen in the dark reaches of the building, in the frightening gloom. When the shop moved to Main Street, the extended family began to arrive. Cousins, nephews, brothers. All of them came from the same small village in China. They came to work in Canada, to cook and serve spicy paper-thin pork, sesame fried shrimp in black bean sauce and platters of transparent rice noodles mildly seasoned so as not to offend the bland prairie palate.

Vivian and I spent each Tuesday and Thursday afternoon in the Chinese restaurant waiting for the last afternoon bus to deliver us home. I would go to drink cup after cup of tepid coffee and smoke cigarettes, furtively at first and then with growing confidence, knowing no friends of my parents would be loitering in The Chinese at such an hour.

Vivian would eat. She told me, while she ate, her father paid her for housekeeping and babysitting after her mother died and she had saved almost four hundred dollars. "It's mostly in the summers," she confessed, "when I don't hardly get to town, Dad in the fields and all."

The Chinese restaurant had been Vivian's idea in the first place. She had been before and said nobody minded if you didn't eat, although eat is what she did every time we pulled open the double glass doors to be swallowed by the dim, spicy interior.

It smelled and looked like an alien world. An aquarium, thick with algae, threw out a murky underworld light and it wasn't until your eyes adjusted to the darkness that you realized paper lanterns, resplendent with dancing green dragons and dangling red tassels, hung over each booth. I had never seen booths before and their intimacy, the semi-circle of dark and tattered vinyl, was instantly appealing.

I talked to Vivian while she ate on those autumn afternoons.

"I'm going to go to Regina when I finish school. I'm going to work in an office. Somewhere swish. Maybe for a lawyer. Or an accountant. Do you think that would suit me?"

And Vivian would nod and acquiesce as she chewed the gristle off a tiny honey-and-garlic spare rib.

"Do you think Margo Tailor is doing it with Alexander Preshinko? I saw them talking in Mrs. Runner's class and Mary MacIntosh — you know, the snob who always wears pigtails — said they were French kissing at her party. In the furnace room."

"In the furnace room?" Vivian paused and considered my question for a moment before starting on a dish of pale won tons floating like gobs of dough in a watery broth dotted with mint leaves and tiny spring onion.

"I'm not going to French anyone until I'm in love. Even then, it's kind of gross, don't you think? I'd rather play volleyball..." and on and on while huge Vivian, with the tiny, beautiful, fine-featured face, ate her way through a mountain of food.

Very few customers came into the Chinese restaurant during the afternoons. Occasionally someone would nip in, accompanied by a blast of cold air, for coffee-to-go, but generally we were alone in the restaurant, except for the slim waiter who served us. I never paid much attention to him when silently he'd materialize. His placid smooth features never changed. He'd always bow slightly and then stand, reed-thin, unsmiling, poised to take our order. Or rather Vivian's order. There was an almost indiscernible quickening in Vivian when the Chinese waiter appeared. Something alert, anticipatory, sprang to her impassive eyes. I was sure it was the thought of food not far off.

She would straighten her back, tug her top over her enormous belly, and without raising her eyes to his, she'd order, smiling a sad soft smile like some submissive Mona Lisa without the mischief.

"A combination number three," she would say, or, when she was feeling braver she'd say something that sounded like *ming yu dong chew.* She spoke carefully, like she was learning a new and magical language rather than reading words off a menu.

It was the waiter, Tong Mark, who introduced Vivian to the more complex culinary delights of his homeland. Soon he was suggesting dishes that might tempt her appetite. Odd things would appear on our table, quail egg drop soups and spongy squid cooked with cashew nuts and fiery red peppers. He would hover anxiously after a meal and pose the all-important question: "You like?" And Vivian, like some fat Buddha well satisfied, would nod, giving Tong the blessing of her pleasure.

"I think he likes you," I told her one day, half-joking.

"Yes," replied Vivian, matter-of-factly, "he does."

I stopped going to the Chinese restaurant with Vivian in the new year. I never saw her pass through the curtains between kitchen and dining area, between East and West, but I know she did. She stopped going to school after Christmas. I didn't really miss her, but occasionally, sitting alone on the bus, heading back home through the bleached grey winter afternoons, I'd remember our secret meetings in the Chinese restaurant and the strange culinary courtship I had witnessed.

It wasn't until spring seeding, when my father and I drove to town to buy fertilizer, that I saw Vivian again. She was working at The Chinese and had grown even bigger than I remembered. She seemed slightly embarrassed to see me when I slipped into the booth we used to share.

"Hi, Vivian," I said with contrived nonchalance. "How's it going?"

"Oh, well," she said, her tiny, plump hands fluttering around the front of her straining smock, "We're getting married, you know, Tong and me."

Dismayed, I couldn't look at her; I couldn't bear to see both the pride and shame playing in her tiny eyes. "Congratulations," I mumbled. "Could I have a chopped egg sandwich and a cup of tea?"

Like a raft riding in the wake of some stately ship, Tong followed Vivian to my table when she returned bearing my sad, bland sandwich. He carried three delicate porcelain cups and a steaming pot of tea.

She spoke to him then, in his own language, and with great care he laid an embroidered cloth across our table and distributed the tiny cups, one for each of us. As she ceremoniously poured three cups of aromatic green tea, Vivian Rumple was transformed from a fat lonely farm girl to a noble matriarch who had learned and mastered some ancient and arcane ritual.

And in the eyes of Tong, her future husband, I could see that she was and would always be the great beautiful woman he had wooed and won in the mysterious and seductive darkness of the Chinese café.

BORDERS

The first time she sees one, actually looks at one, she is on the German autobahn, racing towards France. She hadn't expected it. He seemed like such a nice man, plump and doughy, with a florid face, a sad smile and a large head. He looked like a baby, or at least the way a baby looks in a picture book, mostly because of that big head. And the eyes. He had big eyes, too. Big baby eyes. Those were the things she thought in that brief high-wire second when she had to decide whether or not to get into his car.

Virginia doesn't usually take rides with single men. Women are preferable. They often let her sleep in the car or even take her home to give her a meal, allow her a bath or provide a real bed for the night. They must see in her some shadow of their younger selves. Or their daughters maybe. Yeah, women are definitely the best.

Families are good, too. But not if you're tired. The kids never stay quiet for long. There's that strange hush when she first gets in. If they're young children, they gaze at her level-eyed and knowing. The older ones, told to be afraid of strangers, always turn away, shy. That's usually good for about half an hour before curiosity wins them over. They almost always start yapping away to her if she's in the back seat, amazed that a huge grown person can't understand the simplest things. Sometimes kids will hold up toys and small traveling items and she'll name them in English. *Doggie. Blanket. Cracker.* The kids repeat the words and laugh like she has performed some feat of magic. Even if she's really beat, Virginia will play these games because experience has taught her that families usually go only short distances.

His car was nice too. That was the other thing. He had a nice car and he was going a long way. She hasn't had good rides, just three or four poky little hops between villages. After the last one, she'd asked to be let out near the autobahn. Now that's for people who are really traveling. Like her. She's heading back to Spain. She's going to cross the border in the Pyrenees and say *Hola* to the border guard, dropping the *h* so it sounds just right, the way a local would say it. Bugger the *Bonjour*s and the phlegmy *Goede morgen*s and *Goede nacht*s of the cold Germanic tribes. She wants *buenos* and beaches and afternoon *siestas*. She wants to see those dark men looking, longing, whispering *Rubia chica, hey, hey,* as she swings by to the beach pretending not to understand how much they want her. Yeah, Spain is where she belongs all right, in the heat, near the sea, where evenings are filled with *sangria* and *flamenco*, blood and fire, the promise of passion.

Virginia doesn't actually know anything about passion, but she thinks she does because she's almost eighteen and, heck, she's been traveling alone in Europe for the last six months. She has close to five hundred dollars in her multi-zippered money belt, cash she'd earned working at a nursery in Amsterdam. Not a baby nursery, either, but a plant nursery, a huge automated greenhouse that hired foreigners to do the only thing the machines couldn't. Most of the other workers spoke Arabic and were from countries she had yet to explore: Egypt and Syria and parts of Africa still shrouded in mystery, foreign to Virginia. She hadn't talked to her co-workers much. She had just smiled a lot and gotten down to work, poking the seedlings into the trays, twelve across, twenty-four rows, tray after tray, while the Dutch announcer played sentimental American music on the station they listened to on a tinny portable radio. It was passionless work.

Spain. Now that's the home of passion. It's in the blood. Latin blood, anyway. Antonio is passionate. Antonio, who doesn't speak English but has held her in a tight embrace on the discotheque floor, that's a man with fire in his blood. He wants her. He's crazy for her. Last summer when they were together — or at least sort of together, not actually doing it, but dating — Virginia used to love his wanting her. It made her dance a little bit further away, and she'd smile knowingly, hoping she looked like one of the girls in the American fashion magazines. She was so enticing. That was her power. Knowing about passion but not indulging in it herself.

She's going back to Spain now to reclaim that power, maybe even really get it on with Antonio, if he's back from the military, that is. And if he's waited for her. Maybe they'll even get married because, even though a lot of people don't know it, that's what sex is, actually. A marriage of the flesh.

That's also why she's saved herself. She's been waiting for her husband.

Ever since she was a kid her mother had told her to wait. It's a gift, she'd said, a gift for the man you will spend the rest of your life with. There's another reason you keep your knees together: *Why buy the cow if the milk is free?* When she heard these things from her mom she'd been a kid, dreaming about a husband, who came part and parcel with a white gown and the choir singing like angels and the bells of St. Margaret's tolling out the news that Virginia Kemp had done the right thing, right up to the moment the minister said the words and the rice fell down upon her like manna from heaven. She'd also assumed her husband would be a farmer, what with the cows and the milk and all. Ha! What a re-tard she'd been. Back then she didn't have a clue about the simmering inside, the slow burn, the thing she called passion.

When she'd gotten into the man's car, Virginia hadn't been thinking about passion. She wasn't even really thinking about Spain, even though that's where she will eventually arrive if she keeps on heading south, following this smooth, fast highway. She was thinking about head lice, in fact, because her scalp is itchy and she hasn't washed her hair for three days now.

How do you know if you have them? This isn't the type of question you can ask just anyone. Someone in the hostel in Amsterdam had sent a memo around in five different languages about head lice. As far as she was concerned, that was the last straw. Enough that she had to make beds and wash floors for her room and board after a whole day of twelve across, twenty-four down, row after row. She wasn't going to stick around and have someone else's head bugs leap off a pillow into her hair. No way. Besides, winter was almost over and she was longing for the sun. Only the Spanish sun would do. She didn't want the thin, sickly, indecisive sun of the northern hemisphere.

So she'd gotten into the car. Just when she starts to feel a little bit relaxed and they're really moving, oh, 120 miles an hour or something crazy like that, he pulls it out. When she first sees it, she thinks it's something else, an elbow, maybe, or the pale white fleshy part of his forearm. But no, he's taken his penis out of his pants and he's touching it, rubbing it up and down while keeping one hand on the steering wheel and his eyes straight ahead.

Virginia doesn't know what to do. Briefly, she considers jumping out of the car, but they are going way, way too fast. She'd die for sure. The man remains silent, just stares at the highway and strokes, stares and strokes, so Virginia looks out the passenger window, pretending she doesn't know what he's doing. There's classical music on the car stereo, Wagner, or one of those sad German composers that always make her think of death camps, and because she's scared of the man and the thing that he's doing to himself, she starts to cry. The music swells, the man frantically pulls his penis in time to the music and Virginia watches the grey landscape go by, biting her lip until the world outside the car window is a watery blur.

• • •

She'd gone to Europe because that's what you did when you finished high school. Or, at least that's what the kids who weren't brains or geeks did. The brains went right off to university and the boy geeks got jobs at the concrete plant and the girl geeks at the dog food factory. Then they usually married each other. Cool kids went off to Europe to bum around, hitchhike, discover themselves. Virginia was cool. Virginia was too cool. She changed her name as soon as she got to the little Spanish town where she and her best friend, Rita, were meeting with Rita's older and ultra-cool sister, Linda.

"Call me Gina," she told Rita, once they'd recovered from their jet lag and stopped squealing *Omagawd* at every little foreign thing. "I don't like my name. Virginia. Sounds like, well, you know, like I've never done it."

"But you haven't," said Rita, peering into Linda's mirror, holding her eyes wide as she carefully separated her spiky mascara-thickened eyelashes with a needle. "So it's a perfect name for you. It suits you."

"I don't care. I don't like it and I'm going to be Gina."

Rita smiled, more at herself than at Virginia. "Sure, Gina, whatever you say. Can I borrow your white tank top with the lace front?"

So she became Gina and she and Rita took over Linda's apartment after she went back to Canada to see if she really did want to marry Chester. Rita got a boyfriend almost right away and Virginia would sleep on the beach in the day and dance every night on the discotheque floor, showing off her tan in white clothes that glowed iridescent under the black lights. She would drink *margaritas* until she could feel the power of her blood surging hot enough to move her hips and her breasts to the rhythms of being watched. Watched, wanted, but not taken, never had.

In the late afternoons, changing from her bikini to go out and meet her friends in a sidewalk café, Virginia would stand naked in front of Linda's mirror. She'd run her finger around the three triangles of white flesh, the untouched parts of herself. No one goes beyond these borders, she thought. Not Antonio with the anxious roving hands, not the handsome, black-haired American who gave her the red rose at *Los Cueves Café* and told her she looked like Elizabeth Montgomery, whoever she was. Not even the sun. These parts of her body are what she held back. Why? She didn't know for sure, but they were hers alone.

Rita called her a prude sometimes or, worse, a cocktease. Virginia remembered her coming home really drunk once. She'd had a fight with her boyfriend.

"You okay, Rita?"

"Fucking André."

"What? What did he do?"

"I told him I had my period and so he started dancing with some other chick."

"What do you mean, your period?"

Rita rolled her eyes.

"What does your period have to do with it"?

"Oh, for fuck's sake, Ginny-goody-two-shoes. Turn off the baby blue-eyed bullshit before I throw up."

Then Rita really did throw up and Virginia stayed home from the beach the next morning to look after her, bringing her aspirins and drinks of water and, when she was finally feeling better, fresh avocado mashed on toast.

In the afternoon they talked. Or, at least Rita talked. She talked about André and how great he was. How great in bed. How great it was to have someone make love to you, *like an animal, he was, hungry for me,* but when she saw the blank look on Virginia's face she changed the subject. "Just forget it," she said. "You wouldn't know what I'm talking about."

Try me, try me, Virginia wanted to say. But she knew it was true. She was a virgin. A freak, different from all the initiated people. Especially people like Rita, who were worldly and had sex whenever they liked.

She went into her room where the suitcases lay against the cinder-block wall and took off her clothes again. Her breasts looked like pale jellyfish washed up on a brown beach. Her pubic hair looked like a tangle of seaweed.

Virgin. When she was with men, being a virgin was a good thing. When she was with worldly Rita, it wasn't so good. In the background she could hear Rita on the phone. André and she were talking, making up. Soon they'd be making out. Virginia crawled into bed. It was the middle of the day and the Mediterranean was shimmering like blue cut glass outside the bedroom window.

• • •

The first time she'd been separated from her parents she was just a kid really, but out of elementary school and thinking she was grown up. How old? Seventh grade. Probably twelve, old enough to babysit anyway. And to be on her own. Her parents had gone to England and Scotland for six weeks, some sort of second honeymoon, now that the kids were old enough to be farmed out. Her oldest brother and sister had been allowed to stay at home; a friend of Virginia's father had come to live in the house for six weeks. Her younger brothers had gone together to another family and she had gone to the Dewers', neighbours across the playing field.

She remembers the strange feeling she got seeing her own house across the sloughs and scrappy bits of bush. It was like looking at everything through the wrong end of binoculars. How many times had she looked from her house across to the Dewers' place to see if the kids were out, to see if the lights were on, to see if Joanne or Janet or Margie had left for the bus yet? And even though she'd been over to their house countless times, this was the first time she'd really noticed this backwards view of her own home across the field. How small and quietly contained it looked without her.

It was the same feeling she got when she saw her brothers in the schoolyard. They told her snatched details of their new existence: the Fergusons ate fish every Friday, Mr.

Ferguson played the piano and smoked a cigar every night after supper. They had to go to church. Missing church was a sin.

Then her brothers would disappear into a schoolyard game or hurry off to Mrs. Ferguson's large black car as though the bus lineup was no longer part of their lives, as though they no longer belonged to Virginia anymore. Had they gone on without her?

The Dewers had six children, all girls. Joanne was the eldest, followed by Janet, Margie, Charlotte, Susan and baby Carla, named after Mr. Dewer, who at her birth resigned himself to a state of sonlessness. Virginia made seven. For six weeks in the fall of her twelfth year she was just the seventh Dewer girl, as though one more female child wouldn't make the slightest bit of difference in the jumble of their large, boisterous, emotional household.

To this day, Virginia doesn't know what sort of arrangements were made prior to her parents' departure. She thinks now they should have told her beforehand if money was exchanged. While she was there she worried about who would pay for her groceries or whether or not she should take the money Mr. Dewer gave each of the older girls every Saturday morning. Was she really allowed to eat their food day after day? Did they mind having her there, disturbing the routine of their lives?

Oh, they were nice enough. Mr. Dewer would ruffle her hair and say how wonderful it was to have such a responsible girl in the house. *Mine could take a few tips from you, Virginia. Are you passing on some of those good manners?* And then he'd laugh before disappearing behind the paper. Mrs. Dewer was nice, too. But she was too busy to take any real notice of Virginia's growing discomfort. It wasn't like she wasn't welcomed, but she felt beholden, obliged to pull her weight. She was always on guard, always aware she didn't belong. She offered to babysit as much as she could, trying to pay them back. She tried to eat as little as she could get away with, so as not to be a burden.

Virginia remembers looking over at her house longingly as the weeks went on. She once went over to press her nose against the glass of the back door and see past the hallway into the heart of the kitchen. Boots that she didn't recognize were on the floor. The coat rack her dad made had only one strange jacket hung on it. It looked abandoned. On the kitchen table was a cut glass bowl full of jellied candies.

Virginia walked back across the field to the Dewers' house. The lights were on and no one had closed the drapes. The two older girls were setting the table, the smaller girls were sitting down already. Mr. Dewer held the baby on his knee. Mrs. Dewer was bent over him laughing at something Virginia couldn't see. She slipped into the house and told them she had a stomach ache and could she please be excused from supper? She missed her own family so much the stomach ache was real.

The fire started one of the nights she was babysitting, so technically she was the one responsible. The Dewers had gone out to a barbecue with neighbours. They took a bottle of wine and said they would be back before midnight. Virginia remembers putting the baby to bed first because she was howling the loudest and rubbing her eyes. Joanne bathed the two middle kids and got them into their pajamas. The baby still slept in the Dewers' room. The crib, pushed up against the far wall beyond the rumpled double bed, was like a permanent fixture now with piles of baby paraphernalia stacked around it.

Carla wouldn't settle, so Virginia left a bedside lamp on but closed the door so the bawling wouldn't escape. Babies were such a nuisance. It must have been one of the younger kids who went in later and put the diaper over the lamp to dim the light.

When she finally went to check on the baby, the room was full of smoke. The diaper was burning and the curtains had started to flame. Virginia grabbed the baby and pulled her out of the crib. "Get the kids," she yelled at Joanne. "Get them out. There's a fire." And passing Carla to one of the older girls, Virginia ran to the kitchen and filled a pot with water. When the water hit the lamp, the bulb exploded in hundreds of tiny pieces. It was dark and she was coughing, but Virginia pulled the curtains down and started stomping on them. Each flame that was extinguished seemed to be replaced by two more tongues of fire. She pulled the thick bedspread off the double bed and dumped it on the burning curtains. Again she stomped on it, ignoring the little tiny bits of glass that cut into her feet. There were no flames now, just smoke and water and glass and the stink of a scorched wall, bubbled paint and charred cloth.

Virginia went back into the kitchen. The children were huddled together on the back porch. Two of the smaller ones were crying, but they were all okay. "It's out," she said. "You wait outside. I'll phone." She was shaking when she dialed the number and her voice broke when she asked for Mr. Dewer. When he came to the phone she croaked, "There was a fire..." She listened to the panic on the other end of the line and then nothing. Virginia hung up, walked to the smoky room, opened the window and went outside to wait with the others.

But by the time she got onto the porch they were already there. Neither Mr. nor Mrs. Dewer had shoes on, but they didn't seem to notice that mud was caked on their stockinged feet. They were holding their children, holding all six of them, in a tight circle of arms entwined, bodies pressed together. "My God, my God," Mrs. Dewer was mumbling, reaching out, stroking each of them, affirming their lives, their flesh unscathed, their wholeness. Virginia watched from the porch, feeling the blood sticky between her toes.

• • •

Just a few weeks after she'd made up with André, Rita decided to go back to Canada. André had broken up with her, telling her that he was going to marry another girl, a Spanish girl, and he had to get serious. Rita was mad at first, but soon she was talking about going back to school, too. Maybe get a diploma in Beauty Culture. Virginia hitched to Malaga with Rita to see her off at the airport. She hitchhiked back alone.

She soon realized that the apartment was too expensive for one person, and there weren't so many people sitting at the outside cafés anymore. The tourists had cleared out. Most of the people inside the cafés spoke only Spanish, and even though it made Virginia feel good, like a local, she missed a lot of what was going on.

Once, while she was sipping her *café con leche* and calculating how much longer her money would last, the conversation around her paused and the men sitting nearby looked at her and laughed lewdly, their mouths open and twisted.

After it got too cold to go to the beach and Antonio told her he had to go into military service, she gave notice on the apartment and bought a one-way train ticket to Amsterdam. Someone had told her she could get work in Holland to earn the airfare home.

While the Costa del Sol still shimmered golden in her mind, Virginia headed north. She crossed borders in the dead of night, awakening groggily, grudgingly, to have her passport stamped. She slipped into a babble of languages without bothering to sort them out. When she finally got off the train, she was greeted by winter and the knowledge that she had to find work. And finally, after twelve weeks of working at the nursery planting cyclamen in flats — *Alstublieft, Niets te danken*, and the jabbering Arabic of her colleagues to keep her company — after getting home and washing floors and making beds at the youth hostel so she wouldn't have to pay, she's going back.

• • •

The man with the red face is finished. He's cleaning himself off with a tissue. Virginia wants out of the car. She can't look at him. He's gross. And, yes, he's gearing down, he's moving to the slower lanes, he's going to kill her now, because of what she's seen. She has never felt such fear, and as the car slows, Virginia feels her stomach turn over and rise in her throat. He must know too, because the car shudders to a halt, and he leans over her and pushes her door open. She stumbles out. Some of the vomit splashes on the side of the leather seat and some on the inside of the door. The man swears at her in German and pushes her backpack out too, so it lands in the throw-up.

His tires screech as he pulls away, and Virginia is somewhere in the countryside, miles and miles from the Spanish border. But it doesn't matter anymore. Spain doesn't matter anymore. There is no fire in her blood anymore. The borders are gone. Virginia picks up her knapsack and starts to walk in a direction that will lead her home.

GOING DOWN

In the late fall of 1972, when I was thirteen years old, Marten Hartwell, an experienced bush pilot on a medical evacuation from Cambridge Bay to Yellowknife, fell from the sky to the vast, blank, unpopulated wilderness of the Canadian North. If you have been there, or flown over it as I did in my search for Marten Hartwell, you will understand what this fall means. Somewhere out there were people, tiny specks of people lost among the thousands and thousands of miles of swampy spruce, bedrock, rivers, lakes, the same and more of the same. It goes on forever. I know, because I have seen it.

For the first thirteen years of my life, I lived in that wilderness without knowing its scope, but the autumn

Marten Hartwell crashed, I saw my true geography and was reduced by the sheer enormity of the territory I called home. Reduced and terrified.

Marten Hartwell encountered a freak snowstorm as he flew south to Yellowknife with sick passengers. If he had been blown off his course to the east, he might have been easier to find, for at that time of year the twisted scrap of metal that was his plane and the burnt earth around it would be an anomaly in the empty Barren Lands. But west Marten went, buffeted by winds of early winter, west, way west and then down into the mosquito bogs and the straggly trees, the topography of despair.

The country to the west of my town is a canopy of green, unchanging spruce, unbroken but for hundreds of look-alike lakes. The stunted spruce forests will swallow a man and a plane and a company of sick and injured people quickly. The spruce forest will hide them and then, as time goes on, the snows will come again and bury everything. All evidence is obscured by snow and trees. In an open field, or on a frozen lake, a man could be sighted, but in the trees between the outcrops of rock, shrouded once with that first skiff of snow, it is unlikely anything will be found until spring.

Unlikely became the watchword that swirled around Marten Hartwell and his downed aircraft as our long winter set in. *Unlikely*, said the weary searchers, blinded and dazzled by staring at the same vista for hours. *Unlikely*, said the other pilots, shaking their heads, dumbfounded that yet another of their shrinking fraternity had been sucked out of the sky and hurled to the inhospitable earth. Finding the wreck became unlikely, finding survivors became even more unlikely, and once the snow came to stay, unlikely gave way to impossible.

But still they searched because it was him, Marten, and by God, we knew if anyone could make it, Marten Hartwell, the stuff of legends, could make it.

In the beginning, I helped search for Marten Hartwell and the people who went down with him: the nurse, the sick boy and his pregnant aunt. My Uncle Otto was a pilot and he felt this loss more than others. My cousin Brian and I were both stricken with chicken pox for seven days that fall and, unable to attend school, scabby but not contagious, our energies were no longer appeased with jigsaw puzzles and matchbox cars. To help my mother, Uncle Otto took Brian and me up in his plane three days straight, spotting for Hartwell. It would be good for us to participate, he reasoned. Our eyes were young.

I will tell you without reservation, searching for Marten Hartwell in the dog days of my thirteenth year was the most exciting thing that had ever happened to me in my short and uneventful life. But it was also the first time I saw my landscape and the first time I became afraid.

Brian and I imagined finding them all — the nurse from England, Judy Hill, the boy with the ruptured appendix, David Kootook, and his pregnant aunt Neemee Nulliayok — alive and well. In my fantasy there were always five survivors, for Marten the pilot, the hero of our northern world, not only landed the plane safely but also with the nurse cured the sick boy and delivered Neemee's baby, and they awaited us in some place that resembled the Girl Guide camp at the end of Prelude Lake Road. When we searched, we searched for all of them, of course, but it was Hartwell, more than the others, we wanted to find.

Brian and I spent three days in October lying on our bellies on the deck of a huge open-sided Hercules aircraft as it made low passes over the course Marten Hartwell had charted for his mission of mercy. The mournful drone of those propellers rumbling in our ears reminded us constantly of our task, and, with my uncle, we looked carefully between the trees for the glint of metal, the wisp of smoke, the movement of a human animal, until the monotony of that incredible uniformity became an indistinguishable blur and we could look no longer. Our eyes were young, yes, but our attention span was short, and after the third time up, Uncle Otto decided we had failed to realize the gravity of the search.

For weeks afterwards, at bedtime, just before sleep, I thought of Marten Hartwell alive and impatiently awaiting his rescuers in some muskeg mosquito bog just beyond our eyes, just past the place we looked. He was always close in my mind, and even when the snow came full force and the search lost much of its momentum and no longer dominated the news, I still believed we would find him. We had to look farther, look sharper, have more faith.

But the image that stayed with me after I, too, ceased to dwell on Hartwell and his unlucky crew, was the miles and miles of emptiness I had seen from the belly of that plane. The sameness scared me and I made a promise to myself to see the world beyond those trees and that uninhabited landscape. I simply decided there was more to the world than that horrid sameness, and four years after Marten Hartwell crashed into my consciousness, I walked away from the only place I had ever known. I left home — fled, actually — from the endless winters and my vision of unchanging desolation.

Down I went, down, with the same spiraling, out-of-control feeling that Marten Hartwell must have felt as his Beechcraft careened to the treetops. Down from the top of the world I traveled, to the hot, steaming equatorial centre where nothing was familiar and all was bathed in the light of novelty.

I passed the farmers' markets and the strip malls of southern Canada, passed the sea lion caves and tourist attractions of red cedars and surf. I passed up and over the picturesque streetcar charms of San Francisco and the smoggy sprawl of endless Los Angeles. I crossed the barbed wire border in November and waded through the cheap, tacky allure of Tijuana and beyond to the coastal towns of Pacific Mexico, full of holidaymakers warm with sunshine and tequila.

The language changed, the climate changed, and I felt myself lightened of the burden of my small town. The acres and acres of stunted spruce that had altered my way of looking at the world receded, and were replaced by riotous bougainvillea, blood-red hibiscus and spiky palm fronds. With every mile I put behind me, I felt older and wiser and more and more exotic. Oh, I was a fool, yes, but I was a young fool, fueled by the excitement of the unknown.

At Manzanillo I went inland, to excise my growing disdain of parachute sailors, snorkeling tour guides and beach vendors, the luxuries I could not afford. With the tanned *turistas* I refused association. I was not on holiday, I maintained in faltering street Spanish to anyone who inquired. No, I was traveling. My head swelled, my pocketbook shrank, and still I ventured downward.

After spending two months in Mexico City's Zona Rosa where rice and beans were cheap and plentiful, I tired of the city and headed east to the golden peninsula of Yucatán. With the Gulf of Mexico at my left hand and the green Caribbean sea at my right, I looked off the coast and imagined Havana and Miami and just beyond, just out of sight, the rocky east coast of Canada. Above that, I imagined the Arctic, and I shivered. With the perfume of flowers on the air and the twanging guitar of a wild fiesta nearby, I thanked God for my escape, never once questioning what I was escaping from, or where I was escaping to. With the rash confidence of the young and the foolhardy, I continued to Central America, where wars were no longer rumours, where gunboats ran off the vacant beaches, and khaki-clad soldiers leapt the raw sewage in the streets with unfathomable intent.

In a smoky bar at a Guatemalan border town I played darts and drank whiskey with British soldiers who told me *no, go no further, turn around, retreat,* and because I heard gunfire in the night, at last I listened.

I took a cockroach room in a shabby hotel in Belize City to contemplate my situation. It was not good. With the bulb shining all night to keep bugs away, I watched the weird swaying shadows cast on the grey bedclothes and thought of the sculpted lines of snowdrifts and the eerie green purity of the northern lights. I had virtually no money and had not even contemplated a return journey. I had been traveling for a long time, soaking up experience indiscriminately, learning bad Spanish, living by my wits and the voodoo charms of a tarnished Saint Christopher's medallion pressed into my palm by a French Canadian boy back in Sonora. Like Marten Hartwell as a young pilot, I had been wary at the beginning of my travels. I had guarded myself against danger at every turn, but in that stinking coastal city I let my guard down and like my hero, I, too, was blown off course.

Two days after I started thinking about home, and how to get back there, in a café called Mom's in Belize City in January, 1977, I recklessly took a job to the south, in the pungent jungle near Monkey River. The man who hired me was named Paulo Armando. I had been taking scant meals at Mom's because it was a gathering place for transients and expatriates. I was hoping to find someone driving north, someone looking for a companion, a translator, or just another body behind the wheel.

Paulo Armando was a white face in a sea of black. On the second day, he asked if he might join me for a cup of watery coffee. I consented. He was much older than me, middle-aged, but there was something fierce and burning at his centre and it made me listen when he talked of his hog operation further down the coast.

They needed someone, he said, to care for the animals, to pick up green bananas daily from the United Fruit Growers Co-op on the mainland and to feed them to the pigs, kept just off shore on cayes. They were getting money from an American aid organization in Houston to establish this hog operation in Belize. Growing protein, he called it. Pork for the people. Why didn't I come with him, just to see? The truck was leaving tomorrow, he told me, with fresh supplies and two other young workers, and we could talk more, over a meal, perhaps?

I don't know why I so blindly trusted him, but I did. Paulo had money and connections in the States. His English was excellent, tinged with the slight twang of a cowboy. He was born here, he said, but raised and schooled in Texas. His mother was Belizian, or more properly, British Honduran. He produced a birth certificate and a much-handled photograph from his wallet showing two men with their arms around a smaller, shrunken raisin of a woman. All three were laughing.

Adventure coupled with altruism is an impossibly strong draw. I know that now. I remember Marten Hartwell's flights of mercy. I decided I would go.

Down, further down, we traveled in the back of an open three-ton truck. There were five of us: a hulking black man I would later know as Max, who squatted silent and immobile on a twenty-kilo bag of rice for most of the journey; Tony, a reed-thin mulatto boy, younger even than me, who curled up and seemed somehow to sleep on the jouncing, washboard road; Paulo, in the cab with his brother Roberto; and me. They had offered me a seat in the front but I had chosen the back of the truck. If I was to work I wanted to be with the other workers. I did not want to be singled out, given special treatment because I was a girl, or because I was white, or because the skin on the soles of my feet was still soft. How naive I was, thinking I could melt into that dark sweltering world like sugar into coffee. We traveled only 150 kilometres that day from Belize City to Roaring Creek, a wide spot in the road with nothing more than a collection of shacks, a corrugated Pepsi sign and a gas pump, and then across the Maya mountains to Dangriga. I had never seen land so beautiful. Or towns so destitute. The countryside was verdant, and in the valleys, fields of cane and citrus flourished. From the squawk and squalor of Dangriga we headed south, down the coast, deeper and deeper into jungle.

Inside the truck we maintained the taut silence of strangers except for Max, who didn't speak but sang in his own language. His voice was low and mournful and I wondered if we would bump along that rutted road between mountains and mangrove swamps forever, until we, too, like the sweet notes of Max's song, were swallowed by the pressing jungle.

The shoreline of Belize is swampy, the air close and heavy. Sometimes I think I can still smell it. Darkness fell so quickly that night it seemed the sun extinguished itself in the soupy Caribbean Sea.

We arrived at the water in the middle of the night. A waning moon hung in the sky like some forgotten sack, barely illuminating a launch pulled up, turned on its side, and halfheartedly covered in palm fronds. I thought we must be at the camp at last, but Paulo told me, no, it lay across the water, at the very tip of Placencia Point, a skinny finger of land crooked out and bent inward on itself. It was a ten-minute crossing in a skiff or a forty-five-minute hike down a narrow jungle trail. We loaded the boat in the black night and the five of us crossed the lagoon-like expanse of water to the project.

I don't know if I can tell you how I felt right then, for my travels south were a voyage of desensitization. The extraordinary became ordinary. What was once absurd no longer seemed so. My bizarre circumstances, sharing a boat with four strange men in the middle of the night, sliding silently through the murky, tropical waters to an unseen camp seemed, if not normal, then certainly unremarkable at the time. I must have felt some trepidation, some tremor under my skin, as I realized just how far I had come and how impossible it would be to get back, but if I did, I stifled it.

The next morning — bright, surreal — I saw the pigs for the first time, and that same day I saw our lives on the muddy peninsula were not so far removed from those of the beasts wallowing on small cayes between us and the mainland. They were enormous animals, five sows and two black boars and, removed from the adult pigs to prevent them from being eaten, a litter of sucklings.

Pigs in my experience were sweet pink things living in the clean barns of picture books. These pigs were more horrible than I can describe. The mouth of a pig, snorting and gasping and rooting for food while a steaming hiss issues from between its teeth and tongue, is something I will never be able to forget. They are carnivorous. I used to have to turn away when Max threw them fish heads and whole dead suckers and the bodies of rodents we kept at bay by laying traps across the top of our point of land.

When Tony and I made our daily trek across the water to the mainland to fetch the green bananas, we had to be careful not to get too close to the pig cayes, for they would charge and turn our dugout over in a second with their frenzied feeding snouts. I still dream of being killed and eaten by two black pigs, while in the nightmarish shadows pink sows squeal and stamp their feet with excitement and envy.

Paulo and Roberto did not stay at the camp. They left the second morning. Paulo explained they needed to negotiate a new price on bananas with the United Fruit Growers. I asked to go with them, but he refused, telling me they were allowed to employ only locals, and no one could know of my alien status. They were gone with the truck and the motorized launch for a long time.

Later, when I gained his trust, Max told me Paulo and Roberto went to bribe officials of the banana plantations. Our pig bananas, dumped daily on the banks of the stagnant muddy water, had been skimmed off the top of the truckload bound for market and belonged to the Belizian plantation labourers, who were given product to sell in lieu of wages. The pigs, I learned, ate before the people, while Paulo and Roberto Armando lined their pockets with most of the money they got from their charitable organization.

Or maybe that too was a ruse. I can't say for sure. All I knew was that I was trapped, well and truly trapped, as sure as the pigs were trapped on their cayes. Perhaps the pig farm was a front for something else, guns or drugs or some other illegal thing. With war in El Salvador and Nicaragua and civil strife in Honduras, it was anyone's guess what masquerade our camp played on the edge of that troubled sea. Tony, Max and I were dupes in some strange strategic game where we did not know the rules or even who the players were. But under our stilted shack, where the cook pot bubbled conch and coconut milk, we quickly became an incongruous trio of friends.

Tony and I communicated in broken Spanish. He was a barefoot kid from a village outside Belize City. He told me he had seven siblings still at home, and, before he met Paulo and Roberto, he had been able to take only odd bits of begging money back to the village. He saw the pig farm as an opportunity to make real money. His father worked on a coffee plantation. His mother had worked there too, until she got too sick to work. Now she stayed at home, he said, because she was bleeding all the time.

Those are some of the things he told me about himself, but there are other things I remember about Tony. He was as thin as a featherless bird. He was light brown and wiry. When he smiled, his eyes crinkled and he covered his mouth with his hand because his teeth were rotten. He could maneuver the canoe silently through the water even when it was piled high with bananas and once, while loading the boat, quick as lightning, he pulled a live tarantula spider off my calf and then held my hand as I sat among the bananas and wept.

He knew the names of all the songbirds and could repeat their music. He whistled almost constantly and dreamed of flying. He told me he would come to Canada some day, and even though I know it is ridiculous, I still wait for him. Max was different, older than us, perhaps twenty or twenty-one. He spoke only Creole, more a dialect than a language, and I never really understood that mysterious combination of French and Spanish and English. Tony understood him, and some nights before I drifted to sleep I would hear Max speak my name in the dance of his words. Max hunted and cooked for us.

Each day, mid-morning, when Tony and I paddled across for the bananas, Max went down the path that bisected Placencia Point. His footfalls made no noise. He carried only a long knife, a piece of line and some hooks. Each afternoon

Max returned to our camp with fish or breadfruit or coconuts or birds or pawpaws or mangos, food salvaged from the jungle. With the constants of rice and beans, he made us feasts to nurture our spirits.

Twice I hunted with Max. The first time we all traveled in the canoe to the mouth of Monkey River, where he knocked two iguanas from their treetop perch with avocado pits flung from a makeshift sling. He scooped those prehistoric lizards from the murky headwaters and skinned them there, off the side of the boat. I thought I would not eat them, but cooked all afternoon in coconut milk with seeds of the pawpaw, the meat was as tender and white as chicken.

Another time we left the dugout on the mainland and walked through grasslands, Max with his machete and a flaming torch made of tightly wrapped banana leaves, cutting and burning as we went. The air was filled with smoke and the tangible alarm of small, unseen creatures. We stopped at an inland slough to rest, and Max stripped to his waist and went in, his knife between his lips, and brought four large mud turtles to the surface.

That night, the last before the Armando brothers' return, we three squatted around the cook fire and ate spicy turtle soup from bowls Max had fashioned from their shells. It was that same night, as the dying embers of the fire fell and sent sparks shooting up against the raised floor of our sleeping hut, that Max sang for the second time his strange and beautiful melancholic songs.

That night I knew if I was ever to get out of that country alive, I would have to play Paulo and Roberto Armando against each other. My only weapon, my bribe, was my body. And I decided I had no choice but to give it to them, in tiny frozen pieces, an exchange for flight.

• • •

They found Marten Hartwell on December 9, 1972, thrity-two days after his plane was blown 154 miles off course in a blinding snowstorm. He was the only survivor. Unlike the others, the boy, David Kootook, lived through the horrendous impact of the crash but died later of starvation and, according to some, a broken heart.

My mother, a nurse, was working in the Stanton Yellowknife Hospital emergency ward when they brought Hartwell in. She came home that night grim-faced and resolute. *He only lost his toes*, she told me, *they only had to amputate his toes*. She didn't tell me about the nurse, Judy Hill, and how both thighs had been carved away to the bone and consumed at the crash site, but, of course, I heard. We all heard.

I remember seeing the photograph that appeared the next day in our local paper. It was snapped under the glare of airport lights as they unloaded Marten Hartwell's stretcher onto the tarmac. He was half-sitting, propped on his elbows, and his face, though gaunt and grey, was smiling. As they brought him in through the swirling snow, Marten Hartwell was holding his forearms in the air, extending two fingers of each hand in the shape of a vee. When I saw that photograph many years ago, before I knew anything about survival, I thought those were the vees of victory. For wasn't he victorious against the unimaginable cold, the isolation, despair and fear he must have felt during those days in the frozen muskeg forest? But now I believe something entirely different. I believe the fingers Marten Hartwell held up were signs of peace, a personal peace he had been forced to make with himself, with the animal that would not die.

LIFE'S CHAOTIC SPLENDOUR

The knowledge of her own impending death descends the day after she buys the will. She doesn't actually buy the will, she buys the services of a lawyer. And, in fact, she doesn't buy those services outright, either. She wins them, a lowball bid at a silent auction. Lil doesn't intentionally decide *Time for a will*. She doesn't look through the Yellow Pages or contact more responsible friends who have always had wills, to ask them the how-tos and wherefores of hiring a lawyer to write down the sad list of assets and credits, notarize it, and stash it away in a small locked box until...well, until it's needed. No, that isn't really her style.

She has always intended to have a will, of course, but somehow the very things that demand she possess this legal document — the birth of the children, Honor and Zoe, the purchase of the decrepit but much beloved house on Third Avenue — prevents her from doing it. There just isn't time.

When Honor was born, the thought of a will crossed Lil's mind but it seemed morbid somehow, too much in contrast to the celebration of birth with the fizzy fake champagne, the beribboned christening gown and little Honor's feet sticking out, all pink and wiggling.

They bought the house just before Zoe was born, and by that time, Lil was fed up with lawyers. It wasn't that she didn't like their lawyer. He was a nice enough man, monotone and appropriately clad in trust-inspiring pinstripes, but he charged so much for doing so little it irritated her. They had spent every last penny on the down payment for the house and when he quoted closing costs, she thought she'd lie right down on his big boardroom table and deliver Zoe then and there, just to make sure he earned his paycheque.

So the two small squalling babies and a relentless mortgage inevitably dispels thoughts of forking out for a will. The idea gradually fades, as life, in its chaotic splendour, swirls around Lil and leaves her breathlessly gasping at the rapid passage of time.

The babies grow, the house accumulates more clutter and Lil and Fred live happily on the edge of utter disorder.

Lil buys the will at a fundraiser for Honor's school. She personally despises fundraisers. They bring back memories of sequestering herself in her room and eating box after unsold box of chocolate almonds and Girl Guide cookies and then having to spend all her saved and future allowances to pay back the school or the swim club or the Brownie pack or whoever it was who gave out sweets and the unsound advice to flog them at the doors of strangers.

In those days, Lil had been hopelessly and impossibly shy. Shy and plump. Those were her mother's words, her euphemisms. Fundraising didn't help. If she hadn't been too shy to do her fundraising work, maybe she wouldn't have eaten all those almonds. If she hadn't eaten them, she wouldn't have been plump. The plumper she got, the more shy she became. No wonder she so resented the fundraising racket.

Regardless, Honor's school needs to do it, and Lil dutifully responds as any good parent would. At least it isn't selling. Instead it's to be an auction and potluck supper. She makes an extravagant Malaysian curried noodle salad with fresh parsley and red peppers and decides to donate three cross-stitch samplers that her mother-in-law gave her early in the marriage when she still believed Lil was the type of woman who often wore pink and always matched her handbag to her shoes.

The samplers are nice. They read "Home," "Welcome" and "Love" in powder blue petit point and each word is entwined with a dusty pink rosebud. Nice, but nice for someone else.

When she first got them, Lil hung the samplers on the door. Love. Welcome. Home. She did it for Fred, who in those early days worked night shift at the plant, but the first morning after he came into the kitchen wearily slamming the door behind him, the Home fell off, leaving Love Welcome, a phrase a little too suggestive should the meter reader or the postal carrier be in the mood. Besides, Lil hadn't really liked them that much and had hung them only so as not to offend her new mother-in-law. Now they go to the school auction.

The will, like the samplers, is also donated by a parent. It sits out on the viewing table, a conspicuously official-looking letter offering the highest bidder, the bearer, a free individual will, or in the case of a couple, something called a back-to-back will. *The way we sleep these days*, Lil thinks, when she first considers buying the will.

She pays sixty dollars for it, good value, she is assured by the school principal, who is collecting the money. Good value considering everyone needs one, and he and his wife have paid at least two hundred dollars for the same service.

During the auction, when she is sure hers is the winning bid, Lil tries to work out which one of the parents is the lawyer who signs himself P.T. Kent. A tall man with silvery hair and a well-cut suit at the next table is maneuvering Jell-O into the mouth of a toothless baby. He's a possibility. And, notices Lil, between the long-drawn-out baby bites, he's eating a large portion of curried Malaysian noodle salad with gusto. Must be the one.

The next morning she phones Cheryl, P.T.'s efficient secretary, and arranges a time when she and Fred can come in to discuss the details. Lil feels quite efficient herself as she puts down the telephone and makes a fresh pot of coffee. That's when it hits her. She suddenly sees herself dead, in a coffin. She doesn't imagine it, like a flash through her mind. She *sees* it like a movie. A movie of her death. In the vision, Zoe and Honor are grown girls, and they're scrapping about shoes.

Honor looks to be about twenty-eight. She is thin and graceful. Maybe the ballet lessons have come to something after all, thinks Lil. Honor's face is scrunched up and bright red, and she is speaking to her sister in a tone quite unbecoming for a funeral home. But wait, they aren't in a funeral home. They're in the kitchen of this house. There is coffee dripping through a filter. Lil is there, but not there, somehow.

"I'd suggest you go out and buy some, then," says Honor, holding between thumb and forefinger a down-at-the-heel navy pump. "You can't wear these. They're disgusting." She drops the shoe to the floor.

"Shopping?" Zoe is incredulous. "You want me to go shopping today? I can't believe you. The funeral is in two hours and you want me to go shopping?" She starts to cry and Lil makes a mental note to cut back on Zoe's sweets. She is really, really weeping. She looks a little like Lil does now, actually, a little on the, dare she say, plump side. Still, that's tender, isn't it? Her youngest daughter is too upset to shop for new shoes on her mother's death day. And, how typical of Honor to be so concerned about appearances and public opinion.

Lil shakes her head, mystified that her eldest could even conceive of a mall on such a tragic day, when, suddenly, she's back, very much alive, in her kitchen. The coffee is gurgling and there is a note in front of her, penned in her hand: *Tell Fred about will.* Yes, of course, she was talking to the silver-haired lawyer's secretary on the phone. What happened? Where has she been? What the hell sort of daydream was that?

Her hands tremble as she goes to the coffee machine, refilling her mug. She has seen her own death and her daughters calmly discussing what to wear to her funeral while she lies dead in a box. It's unthinkable. Lil sinks into a kitchen chair and does some quick calculations on the scrap of paper before her. Honor is six. In the vision she looked twenty-eight or so, twenty-eight at the outside. That only gives her two more decades. She'll die young. Oh, my God, it's a tragedy. Lil can't stop herself. She puts her head down on her arms and starts to weep.

She pulls herself together when the doorbell rings. It's some skinny kid selling chocolates to send the band to Quebec City. Wouldn't you know it? Lil buys two boxes and devotes the next ten minutes to meditations on death, chocolate and the futility of exercise. She cracks a bottle of red wine when the chocolate is gone. *Might as well live it up now,* she thinks, and by the time the children come home for lunch she's in a tizzy, mumbling about shoes and cemetery plots and the cruel hand of fate.

It happens again later that day, but the second time, Lil has a totally different experience. It's a memory that comes to her, rather than a vision, but the memory has been so long submerged it feels like a revelation.

Lil is a very small girl, younger than Honor, three perhaps. Yes, she's three-and-a-half. She knows this with certainty because adults laugh at her solemn proclamation *I'm free. Free-and-a-half.* Her grandmother has died. Lil knows this because of the funny way the old woman was breathing in her wheelchair and the weird light that was coming off her body.

She hadn't wanted to nap because she could tell something was going to happen, but the excitement overcame her and she did sleep. When she woke up her mother was in the sleep-smudged room telling her that Grandma had gone away. Her mother had red eyes and she didn't say the word dead. Lil knew Grandma was dead, however, because in the dream, in the deep nap dream, she was sitting on the porch of her grandmother's house in Nova Scotia and surrounding her were hundreds and hundreds of butterflies who were all her grandmother. They fluttered and skirted, lighting briefly, each more beautiful than the last, kissing her face, her brow, the tip of her nose, and then they were gone. She tried to tell her mother about the dream, but she was shushed and held too tight for a while before being left to the haphazard care of an out-of-town aunt who spoke in hushed tones, drank sherry and told her mother to *Cry, cry, let it all go, cry.*

This memory comes back to Lil as she is vacuuming the living room. It comes back to her with the intensity of the coffin/shoe-shopping vision and she has to sit down on the maroon sofa to collect herself. Maybe she's a prophet, one of those psychic people who are born that way, tapped into the Source, so to speak. Maybe she's been corrupted by the ways of the world and her formidable power has only now found its way to the surface? She hasn't thought of the butterflies for years.

Something happened once, though, when she and Fred were courting (if you wanted to call it that). Fred always claims he wooed her, although Lil mostly remembers lying in his single student bed, naked and excited and calling out to him, only to hear, "Be there in a second." Eventually she'd put on one of his shirts and make her way out to the living room where Fred and his buddy Wayne would be watching the late news or the late late news or the movie after the late late news. T-shirt tight around her rump, she'd curl up next to Fred on the slouched sofa and watch Jimmy Stewart or Laurence Olivier — now there were a couple of men who knew something about wooing — until the test pattern drove them all to bed.

The weird thing happened around the same time her girlfriend Andrea Jenkins told her the best way to get a man's attention was to ignore him. Fred had phoned her, hoping they could get together, and using an Andrea Jenkins technique and a voice that wasn't really her own, Lil had informed Fred she wasn't available to *hang out* with him anymore. She'd further informed him that he should have something specific in mind — a date — before he called. Then she'd weigh her options and see if she could accommodate him.

The stunned silence on the other end of the line should have told her just how far she'd overstepped and how hurt Fred felt by her chilly retort, but did that stop her? Oh no, not with Andrea Jenkins' words about Fred taking advantage and Fred presuming so much echoing in her head like some sort of evil mantra. "I think we'll have to see less of each other, Fred. You know, leave our options open."

"Yeah, well, what about tonight?"

And Lil's reply, patiently condescending: "What *about* tonight, Fred?"

"Ah, Lil, forget it. You call me sometime if you want, okay? I'll be around." And he'd hung up the phone, leaving her sick and scared, like someone had just driven a spike through her heart. Would she have to go around for the rest of her life pretending to be some perky co-ed with open options when all she really wanted was Fred? All she'd ever wanted was Fred, the guy she could relax with, the tall gangly guy who made her laugh and loved her to pieces.

Later that afternoon Lil knew what she had to do. She had to get to Fred before he went out. Saturday night was pressing upon them and unless he was pining for her in some dark room, which she sincerely doubted, he'd go out to one of the pubs to play darts and drink pints with his friends. Without Lil there, he might even try talking to another girl, and who wouldn't be won over by the slow, sweet voice and that gentle, shy grin?

A catch formed in Lil's throat as she hurried towards Fred's place, knowing she'd have to cross the river on the train bridge if she was going to get to him before the Andrea Jenkinses of the world snagged the only person she'd ever really cared about. Cursing Andrea and crying for Fred, Lil struggled up to the tracks behind the art gallery. Fred lived on the north side of the river. They'd walked this bridge before, but always together. Lil hated the unnatural way you had to step on the ties, not quite a full stride but almost, and, even more than that she hated the sight of the water down below. Fred did it all the time because walking the train bridge was the quickest way to campus and the quickest way to her house.

Lil started out, confidently at first. Step, step, step. Where had this wind come from? It was breezy out on the water. Step, step, step. Stupid Andrea Jenkins. Stupid, stupid, stupid. Stupid Me. Fred, Fred, Fred. Step, step, step.

She was more than halfway across when she heard the hooting. It was the train. She was walking the train bridge at four in the afternoon, and she'd totally forgotten about the train. Lil couldn't see it yet, but she could feel it. The trestles were vibrating ever so slightly. What had Fred said when she'd asked *What if a train comes?*

Just move to the side, he'd said.

Oh, my God, move to the side, thought Lil. She stepped over to the edge of the bridge and grabbed one of the steel supports. There was now nothing between her and the water. She trembled on the side of that bridge, clinging to the post while ten thousand pounds of iron flew by, while the engineer hung on the whistle so that her eardrums shriveled and shrank inside her head. Lil was trembling and crying. The bridge was shaking, too. The vibrations subsided. She was still alive. Slowly she opened her eyes, still keeping her entire body tightly pressed against the green iron girder of the bridge. That's when she saw it.

Okay, so it wasn't a butterfly. But it was a moth. A moth was hunkered down on the steel post. It was small, about the size of her thumbnail, but to Lil, that brown and grey creature lying inert on the post was a miracle. It was a miracle simply due to the fact that it was not dead. The teeny feet moved and, as though she willed it, the wings, folded together like prayer, opened a half crack and settled back together. It was alive. And Lil was alive. She was clutching a girder, swaying and trembling over the St. John River, but she was alive.

The butterflies of her grandmother's passing fluttered though her mind then, and she'd hauled herself over to Fred, who was drinking beer in the backyard like nothing had happened. He seemed so glad to see her, and grinned when she told him about the train.

"Way to go, Lil," he said, putting his arm around her. She didn't mention the moth because Fred would have found that a little too weird. She simply stood there, with his arm heavy on her shoulder and knew, just knew, he was the one.

She is still sitting on the sofa, vacuum cleaner plugged in, when Fred comes home after work. He smiles at her without really seeing her, and goes to the kitchen to get a drink of water. Honor and Zoe rush in from the backyard calling *Daddy, Daddy* and Lil hears him pour them drinks too.

He's holding her note in one hand when he comes back. She remembers the calculations, working out the age of the children in her vision, the way her life is just a brief flash and then gone. Lil stands up then and walks over to Fred and puts her arms around him. He smells like chocolate.

"Who's Will?" he asks.

"Oh, nobody. He's nobody," says Lil, leaning into him. "Just someone I used to know. But he's gone now. He flew away." Lil starts to laugh, and Fred, not even knowing what the joke is, laughs too.

RUBBER BULLETS

Couple of weeks ago some Japanese tourists mistook my husband for the President of the United States. He's golfing, see. Somewhere near the fifth hole (which is really tricky because of the sand traps) this Oriental couple rides up in one of those carts. They're both wearing safari hats and white clothes, the type you see in old movies about the Indian Empire. Bill — yeah, I know, they have the same first name — said later he expected them to have one of those flasks of gin and tonics or saké or something real exotic-like.

Anyways, they drive up to the edge of the green and start jabbering in Japanese like he's supposed to know what they're saying or something. The only thing he understands is the word Clinton. It keeps on coming up — "Clinton,

Clinton" — and he says they're nodding their heads, you
know, sort of bowing, like it is in their tradition, really excited,
even though he tries to tell them, no, he's not Clinton, not
even close.

Anyways, they can't speak any English and he's lined
up this great shot which should keep him under par on the
fifth and he's got a couple of beers riding on it, so he just lets
them go yipping ahead. He's putting. You know, looking
really concentrated and stooped over the golf ball like it's
presidential business or something.

So the little Japanese guy gets out this big camera and
his wife gets out the smallest camcorder in the world and
they start taking shots, footage. And Bill gets all nervous, of
course, and misses his putt but smiles real dignified and
statesmanlike, right at the camera, and they're all oohing and
ahhhing and saying "Clinton, Clinton" and he pops it in
like he meant to do it in four instead of three.

The reason I know all this is he came home afterwards
all excited and told me while he was drinking a beer on the
deck. But the weird thing is, he's telling me, okay, he's sitting
there, telling me, pretty darn full of himself, thinking he
looks like Clinton and all, and I hand him a second frosty
and he looks at it like he's never seen a beer before and asks
me — just as nice as can be, mind — if he can have a glass.
For his beer.

Well, I should have nipped it in the bud right there,
him and his Illusions of Grander or whatever. But, like some
sort of sicko fifties wife I goes and gets him one, even dust
off one of them big German steins with the handle and the
lid and all, the one Ruth's mother brung back for me for
watering her plants and cleaning out the cat box the summer
I was eighteen. Anyways, yeah, so I give the mug to Bill, and
he pours it real careful so it's foamy but not too foamy on

top, and then he holds up this beer like he's on TV, he shows his teeth, all fake and charming, and says cheers. "Cheers, Hillary."

That cracks him up, which kinda makes me mad, 'cause to me he doesn't look anything like Clinton who, truth told, I haven't really paid much attention to, me being Canadian and all. Bill looks like Bill, like a great big radish, with his shiny red face and yellow chompers, but I didn't tell him that. I mean, he was pleased as all get-out, and I figured okay, if some camera-happy tourists want to take home pics of my husband and tell all their hundreds of relatives back home they saw the President of the United States, so what? Right? No skin off my nose.

Now this is the part where it really gets weird. Coupla, three days go by, I'm doing my thing with the kids and all, you know, making sure they don't kill each other while still trying to have a life. So, it's morning. I'm lying on the sofa 'cause I'm really bushed. The Worm was up cutting teeth half the night (We call him The Worm, but his real name is Warren, after Bill's stepdad).

Anyways, I'm lying there trying to get some shut-eye. Millie is in the bathroom playing like she runs a beauty parlour for all her dolls, and The Worm is foraging for the Cheerios I'd scattered on the carpet when the phone rings. Well, that's not so weird, but I get up, all pissed off like, and I'm prepared to blow off Crystalle or Pam or any of the other girls who just need to borrow a cup of raisins 'cause they're right in the middle of making bread pudding and the kids won't eat it without raisins and who can blame them? I wouldn't eat bread pudding any old way or, if I did, I sure the heck wouldn't tell my neighbours I was making it. Poor people's food, bread pudding. For folks who can't afford Jell-O, my mom always claimed.

But it's not any of them on the phone. It's this guy from the FBI. Yeah, I'm not kidding. He says he's from the Federal Bureau of Investigation and at first I think it's some cheesy company trying to sell us a dresser. Like we don't already have enough bedroom furniture. Anyways, he finally says it F-B-I, like the letters, not the words, and I figure I better listen up, find out what the hell's going on. Turns out this guy has seen the pictures, Lord knows how, wants to know if we know a Mr. Teing Fung. Teing Fung, Fung Teing or something like that.

It finally clicks that he's talking about the Oriental guy who took the golfing pictures, so I say, *No we don't know him from Adam. And how did'cha get our names anyhow?* Well, turns out this guy, this Teing Fung or whatever the hell, is being held in Boston as some sort of security risk. Something to do with these photographs of Bill, my Bill, but the FBI fellow wouldn't say anything else, 'cept he'll be in touch. Well, I hang up then, mouth hanging open and The Worm, who's mad I've been on the phone, has practically chewed through the phone cord. I'm shocked. I'm just shocked stupid.

Bill comes home that night and I'm busting to tell.

"FBI phoned."

He doesn't even look up from the chainsaw he's tinkering with out on the deck. "Oh, yeah? What she want?"

"She?" I just keep drilling him with my eyes.

He looks at me then, all puzzled. "Who phoned?"

"FBI," says I. And then I repeat it real slow so it sinks in: "Federal Bureau of Intelligence. Americans. The muscle who go around in suits and blow up things. You know, James Bond."

Well, I could tell I've gone a little too far 'cause Bill just looks at me, dumb as a doorknob. "Huh?" he says, wiping the grease from the saw on the back ass of his second-best jeans. I don't say nothing though, just smile. "They're gonna phone back."

When I see him scowl, I suddenly get scared. "Bill, you didn't do nothing, did you? Something you're not saying?"

"No," he says, real slow, so I believe him with my whole heart. "We still got any of that chewing tobacco round the house?"

Well, me, I can't wait for the FBI to ring back. Every time the girls call with news about their cat's kittens or little Jimmy's boils or some gossip about the paving crew that's in town and raising everyone's hormones sky high with their tight, tarry jeans, I have to practically bite my tongue off so as not to tell. I tell Millie, though, mostly because she's three and I just gotta tell someone. "Your daddy," I say, right proud, "your daddy is wanted by the FBI."

Turns out I'm right.

They want Bill — my Bill — to stand in for the President of the United States when he goes on his tour to someplace in Africa. Turns out there are some American soldiers down there — been there for a long time. They need some encouragement and Mr. Clinton needs some good press. Problem is terrorists. Jungle terrorism. It's dangerous down there in this unpronounceable African place. Too dangerous for Mr. God Almighty Presidente himself, but, heck, not too dangerous for my look-alike husband. I guess them soldiers haven't seen Mr. Clinton before, at least not up close and personal like, so if he looked a little like my radish man, heck, they wouldn't know the difference. Folks on TV'd be fooled too, according to the FBI muscle.

"Leave it to us, Mrs. Freeman. Leave everything to us."

Then they told me about the money. I just about lost it. Get this. All expenses paid plus ten thousand dollars a day. Double for the time Bill's actually walking around in Congo-Bongo. It's close to forty thousand dollars American. For three days. Imagine!

It's so much money it makes me feel sick and I have to sit down and pull The Worm up onto my lap, just to get readjusted to reality. He's damp and drooling and his cheeks are bright red from the molars breaking through but, despite that, he smiles and crows when I blow air onto his tummy to make his favourite farting sound.

"Forty grand," I say, blowing hard onto his lovely soft skin. "Forty grand. Three days, peanut! Just three days." And then I blow again until he's laughing so hard he spits up on the couch.

The pressure's on like never before. Bill is all anxious and drinking too much, trying to decide if he'll go. The Yankee muscle, CIA, has already done a security check on him and they've made him sign a paper that keeps everything hush-hush. He's not allowed to talk to anyone except me. Ha! As if.

He's all clammed up tight as a Scottish wallet thinking about the money on the one hand and on the other, some spook jumping out of the jungle with a machine gun and spattering his guts all over deepest, darkest Africa. I just let him stew.

"Do what you want, hon. Me and Millie and Warren are right behind you, no matter what," I say. "If you don't want to go, stay right here and we'll just kiss this one good-bye right here and now." I make a big smack on my palm and blow it off like forty grand had no more weight than a dandelion gone to seed. And then I get a little softer 'cause I see he's all ripped up over wanting to make us a better life, get me a dishwasher and maybe pay off the truck and I says, "Heck, Bill. It's not like we weren't happy before."

The next day, the day the American envoy person is going to call back to confirm Bill's decision, something happens, something that almost makes me believe there is a God who watches over even little ol' us.

This is it, see. Bill's taken the day off, called in sick 'cause he really is sick — with anxiety, that is. So he's not talking and he keeps saying *Yeah, I'm going*, then, next half hour, *No, I'm not going*, and he keeps on looking at me all moony like he's going to die or, if not like that, then all slitty-eyed and suspicious like all I care about is money, until I'm sick to death of it.

"Go mow the yard, Bill," I tell him. "Grass is as high as a cow's tits and you might as well do something useful, especially if it's the last thing you ever do round here." He doesn't hear that last bit, which is a good thing considering his state of mind, being so on the fence and all. He just does like I tell him to, hauls out our old John Deere, the one Bill's stepdad gave us before he moved to the retirement home. He starts her up and starts mowing, round and around in circles, getting smaller and smaller with every pass.

Now we don't have a big yard, but it's country out here, so we keep almost an acre mowed so the place looks good and presentable from the road. Anyways, Bill's mowing and sweating in the sun 'cause, typical, he's forgot his hat, and he's turning redder and redder and more and more tense about the big decision, when all of a sudden I see the Worm out in the grass just in front of the mower.

I'm standing at the window, washing the dishes, when I sees his round bald head and a bit of his arm sticking up out of that tall grass, probably cooing and drooling at his dad as he comes towards him on the riding mower.

"Warren! Warren! Bill!"

I scream it loud through the window, but he doesn't hear over the mower. I can see it all happening and I can't do nothing to stop it.

"Bill!" He's not watching, he doesn't see. And there is Warren's bald head and the blades are whirling, grass clippings flying, and I watch, a scream dead in my mouth as the mower grinds towards his sweet flesh. It doesn't stop. The blades swallow my little boy, and the linoleum comes up in a split second and I'm somewhere gone.

Next thing you know, it's drool wakes me up. Yeah, drool. There he is crawling over my face, The Worm, just as whole and healthy as you please. I can't believe it. I look around for marks and blood and the razor-thin lines of the mower blade, but there's nothing. There's some wailing in the background, but Warren is there on top of me, pawing me, cherry-cheeked and slobbering, sort of laughing to himself like his momma on the floor is weird but good, too. I pull him down and feel his hot neck and smell his beautiful boy pong and I'm crying and laughing and saying his name over and over…Warren, Warren…like I'll never stop saying it.

The screen door slams and it's Millie holding a shredded rubber dolly and crying like someone just told her all her birthdays now and forevermore are cancelled. Bill's right behind her holding a part of the plastic baby's leg with the little toes like spaghetti and the foot all mangled and mashed and I can tell he's kind of apologetic but kind of pissed off too.

"What are you two doing?" he asks, like he's suddenly noticed The Worm and I are lying together in a big tight knot on the floor crying and laughing, all snot and tears.

"We're staying," I say. "We're all staying right here."

Bill looks at me, kind of wondering what he's heard, and what I mean, but Millie knows. She piles on top of Warren and me and pulls her daddy halfway down with her. "We're staying here, Daddy," she says, all solemn-like. "We're all going to stay here."

And I know he knows, and it makes me so damn happy I grab at his big red mitt and pull him down on top of me, too, gentle though, so we don't crush the kids, and the four of us lie there in the middle of the kitchen floor clutching bits of pink rubber and grinning like the fools we'd almost been.

RAISING CADE

I am lying awake listening to the sound of my husband Mike snoring and the sound of rain on the roof. Both are familiar, neither comforting. In fact, I am not listening to either of these things. I am listening for something that is not there. I am listening for the sound of my son coming home. I am listening for the opening of the door, the thunk of his boots, and the rasp of his coat shucked off his shoulders and flung, not hung, across the back of a kitchen chair.

If he comes now, I will gladly hang his coat up in the morning. I will not scold. If he comes now, I will let him sleep late, let him turn his music up loud, give him space.

But he does not come, and the clock by my bed tells me only one thing: he is now four minutes later than last time I looked.

I will kill him when he gets home. I will wring his scrawny irresponsible little neck. I will ground him. For a week. For a month. Forever. How dare Mike sleep? How dare he sleep when our son, our only child, is out there in the rain, two hours and twenty-six minutes past his curfew?

Yet it is small wonder he sleeps and I lie awake brooding. We have always been like this, chalk and cheese, as different and sometimes, I think, as far apart as the sun and moon, unable to inhabit the same sky without stealing each other's light.

I am an artist. I paint watercolours. I have a small following, and I exhibit and sell my work in a number of Canadian galleries. I make a modest income from painting and have been asked recently to do a retrospective of my work. Mike is a hydrographic engineer. He also works with water: aqueducts, sewage systems, water purification plants, you name it. At very least, we have water in common.

After we were married I found out many of our friends had made wagers on whether our marriage would last. You know, "Three years. No, I'll give them five," that sort of thing. So now that we've been together for sixteen years, I'm almost smug about it. And really, why shouldn't I be? Sixteen years is a long time with the same man, and the fact is, we're still pretty happy. Our son Cade has a lot to do with that, but it also goes to show that opposites do attract and when you marry someone who isn't the least bit like you, an awful lot of years go into just figuring them out.

We were living in Bermuda when Cade was born. That's important, because moving to Bermuda was the only reason Mike and I got married in the first place. I mean, we loved each other and all, but we were perfectly happy living together in our little flat on Queen Street above Pooch Parlour, the dog grooming shop run by Lance and Miguel, two drag queens intent on beautifying all creatures canine. They gave us a cut on the rent because when it was busy, and even when it wasn't, the apartment always smelled like wet dog.

So when Mike was offered a great job building a reverse osmosis plant in Bermuda, we had to either break up or get married. They would fly me down only if I was Mike's spouse. Bermuda, it turned out, was more conservative than my husband.

We talked it over and went out that night for Chinese food and a marriage licence. I got all dressed up too, thinking we could do it after the bok choy and beef, but they made us wait twelve hours after buying the licence, in case we changed our minds. So two days before we flew to Bermuda, Mike and I went to the Justice of the Peace. It was pretty painless, actually. We bought a bottle of champagne afterwards and took it home to drink while we finished packing. Miguel and Lance brought up a six-pack and some flowers they were planning to send to someone whose dog had died. The woman who was moving in came over just as we popped the cork, so she went back downstairs to order a cheese and anchovy pizza and to pick up another bottle of champagne. We had a little party.

Mike, I remember, wanted to unpack glasses and utensils, but we talked him out of it. He got into the spirit of things after a few glasses of champagne, and we ate stringy pizza with our hands, passed the bottle around and made crazy toasts to the future, to friendship, to marriage.

Cade is fifteen now. He's a great kid, just the right combination of Mike and me. He got the best of both of us, Mike's sense of responsibility tempered with my sense of fun. He's got my wild imagination but Mike's stick-to-it-iveness, and his enthusiasm for a project, no matter how bizarre, doesn't seem to wane. Cade doesn't leave things half finished the way I do, but he doesn't sweat the details either. He's a kid with the big picture.

I'm telling you this because Cade is important to us. He's our raison d'être, justifying all the hard times and the misunderstandings and the compromises that have made up these sixteen years of marriage. I know the psychologists would pooh-pooh a couple putting so much emphasis on a child. They would see him as responsible for propping up a shaky relationship. I think that's rubbish.

So where the hell is the little shit? He's gone out with some friends to a beach party, and he's late. Mike and I have been married to each other for sixteen years and he's fast asleep. Despite the rain, despite the time, despite my concern, he's lying here beside me dead to the world, drooling on the pillow.

After we surprised ourselves by moving to Bermuda and almost immediately conceiving and having a son, we had to get down to the serious business of deciding how to raise him. I was all for experience. I wanted Cade to experience everything. I wanted to take him everywhere, introduce him to the big, beautiful world that had suddenly opened up since our move.

I remember putting his little hand on the smooth, shiny skin of a tropical toad just so he could feel it. I put bougainvillea flowers in his hair and smushed mango on his lips before he was ten weeks old. I wanted his world filled with wonder. I wanted everything for that child. I wanted it all.

Mike had some different ideas. He felt we should be careful with Cade. I guess he couldn't get over our making this fragile thing, a mysterious, tiny creature who was helpless against the world. Mike is big on responsibility and he felt an overwhelming responsibility to the child we had brought into the world.

"He's not a plaything," he'd admonish me, as I'd throw Cade up towards the coconut palms and catch him, gurgling and laughing. Or: "He needs a hat." Or: "Don't let him do that," as our small son started pulling himself up on furniture or mucking about in my paint box while I absently tried to capture the exact once-washed grey of the craggy coral shores. Mike spent one beautiful Saturday morning taping foam rubber on the edges of our furniture so no injury would befall our son, should he stumble. I'm sure if Mike had had his way, Cade would have been wrapped in cotton wool and coddled in a darkened room.

And where were we, while Mike patiently plugged all the electrical sockets and put baby-proof locks on the cupboard doors? Oh, probably out in the garden admiring the markings of a venomous snake or feeling the tickle between our toes of what we thought was grass but was actually poison ivy. Doing something innocently simple, something silly, something Mike would call careless.

I can't begin to tell you how much pleasure I took from those long tropical days when my new baby and I had nothing better to do than to get to know the island and each other. It was a magical time, and even now, as I lie in bed, thousands of miles away in a colder climate, I can still remember how it felt to be young and so in love with a creature of your own making.

The worst rows we had, Mike and I, were about the baby. If Mike was overprotective, as I claimed, then I was the opposite: irresponsible, feckless, undependable, wild. He questioned my ability to mother because I insisted on doing the exact opposite of everything the baby books told me. Formal naps were dispensable. Cade napped wherever we happened to be, whenever he was tired: in the buggy, on the beach, and once on the hood of a car while an impromptu reggae party sprang up around us, thick with the smell of hashish in the summer heat. Mike thought I should change my life to suit Cade's and that schedules, predictability and consistency were important in a baby's world.

I understand now what he meant, but at the time I saw his parenting approach as a way to trap me in that hot, airless apartment twice a day, to make me more, well, traditional, the type of wife and mother that required no explanation to conservative colleagues.

Cade has survived our differences. And our opinions, over time, have mellowed. Tonight it seems our roles are quite reversed. Here is the overprotective father, fast asleep, while the carefree and careless mother frets and tosses in the early hours of morning waiting for her boy to come home.

I wonder, briefly, if he is dead. I wonder if there has been an accident and even now they are trying to identify his body. I see some man in a white coat thumbing through the phone book, looking up our number: "I'm sorry to inform you, there's been an unfortunate —" But the phone is mercifully and terribly silent.

There was an incident at another beach, many years ago, that sealed me to Mike forever. Having our baby did that, yes, but I was still prepared at different points in those early days of motherhood to pack Cade up and take him back to what I considered my real life, my former life in Toronto. When Mike looked at the magnificently turquoise sea around us as an engineering equation, an infinitely perplexing question of desalination and purification, mentally I would be packing my bags. Enjoy it, I wanted to scream. Don't analyze it. Enjoy it.

Friends came to visit when Cade was eight months old. Aria, tall and blonde and bony, exhibited at the same gallery I did, and years before we'd gone to art school together. She came to Bermuda, she told me, to gawk at my domesticity, play mommy with my baby and get a tan. Aria had with her a handsome and totally smitten young art student, Roger. They came for a week.

On our second day together I took them to one of the beaches on the south side of the island where enormous sweeps of sand meet the sea. It was sunny and warm and, being mid-week, there were very few people on the beach. Mike was working, so it was just the three of us stretched out on a blanket, and Cade snoozing under a beach umbrella.

We lazed in the sun, caught up on gossip, ate an enormous picnic lunch before anyone was really hungry, and simply lounged, drinking ginger beer and laughing at our indolence. Cade woke up, nursed, and after that was all bright smiles and gurgles. Aria held him, played in the sand with him and generally agreed that yes, he was utterly compelling, the most beguiling, cutest baby she'd ever laid eyes on. She said all the right things, and I remember being filled with pride and overall goodwill for the world.

We went into the water, Aria first, and then me, carrying Cade. I'd stripped his clothes off and he was naked in the sun, dangling his feet in the water as the beach fell sharply away. We didn't go far from shore, just enough so the waves would break in front of us and I could jump through the surge of water holding Cade in front of me. He loved the movement of it, the great swoosh and swirl of the warm water breaking around us. We twirled and my back was to the ocean. Aria, who fancies herself a swimmer, was farther out, diving and playing in the surf. Roger was on the beach, propped up on his elbows, watching us, when it hit.

I had heard of them, of course. You can't live on an island long without hearing of rogue waves, monsters that form far off the coast from some underwater disturbance and rise, gathering speed until they crash against the shore.

It took me by surprise. Maybe Roger saw it coming, maybe Cade himself looked at the tower of water with gleaming anticipation. I don't know, but I do know the huge wave crashed down on top of us and pulled him from my arms so quickly and with such force I had no hope of hanging on. He was naked and slippery as a fish, and in a second, as I was flung upside down in a torrent of water, he was gone. My infant son was gone.

I was helpless against the ton of water that grasped me, stripped my bathing suit from my body, tossed me, weightless to the shallows of the beach. I rose unsteadily and screamed, "He's gone."

Roger was on his feet already, half into the water, and we both rushed out into the still-churning mass of effluent foam. My hands groped the bubbles, broke the sluicing surface to find him below. Down and down again I plunged, wild with horror, but only water infused with air flowed through my grasping hands. Empty. An unholy howl that I do not remember came from my mouth, from the emptiness of my hands, and somehow I registered the impossible sun still anchored in the sky while my Cade was sucked away below the surface of that envious turquoise sea.

I don't know how much time went by or how long he was under water. Perhaps it was no more than a minute or two, but I know it was long enough for my world to be forever tempered with the knowledge of loss. And then, when I knew he was gone forever, I saw him surface near Aria and I lunged to the spot and felt his firm flesh at my fingertips. I pulled Cade out of the sea by his neck and shoulders, the same way he had been pulled from my body. He sputtered, gasped and turned bright red, wailing with the indignity and shock of it all. Together, we staggered up to the beach and I clutched him against me, sobbing and shaking so badly my legs would not support my weight and I sank into the warm sand. Roger told me later the first thing I said, as I lost my footing and collapsed, was, "Don't tell Mike."

I did tell him, of course. I had to. I remember leaving Cade with Aria and Roger and driving to the other side of the island, waiting for Mike outside the waterworks plant. I was still sick with anxiety, and I started to cry as soon as he came out of the building dressed in his ridiculously bright Bermuda shorts and blazer. Mike listened wordlessly as I told him how close Cade had come to being sucked out to sea.

When I had, at last, finished, my husband spoke. "He would have come back," he said simply. "He would have come back on the seventh wave."

He mentioned parabolas and the angle of waves bouncing off a curved surface at a given axis. "And babies close up, you see. They won't try to breathe when they're surrounded by water. It's instinctual. They think they're still in the womb." He blushed then, and added, "I read it in one of your baby books."

I knew at that moment I loved him, and what I loved in him was his cool rationality, his simple faith in facts. I knew also that we were good for each other, and we would spend the rest of our lives giving the other what they needed.

And as though he has timed it, I hear the front door open and Cade slip quietly back into his family. Mike stirs, mumbles something about gravitational fields, and snores again. I curl into his solid warmth and drift into sleep.

AUTUMN FIELDS

The station wagon is packed to the roof, the hatch barely closing. My husband, Tom, has cleaned the garage, something I've been after him to do for weeks, and now damaged sheets of drywall, a tricycle with two wheels, bits of scrap plastic, a cracked garden hose, an old bureau with no drawers and my pram, my corduroy-covered, hooded, huge, old-fashioned, sagging workhorse of a perambulator are on their way to the landfill.

"Want to come to the dump?" he asks, rubbing his gloved hands together in anticipation.

"You've got the pram."

"Oh, that." He steps towards me, torn between comforting and cajoling. "It's done its time, Jeannie. It's served us well. You know yourself, the springs are shot on one side."

Of course he's right. Natalie and Jen, the twins, used to stand on the rails and hang on while I'd wheel Will down the road. They loved riding shotgun like that, leaning forward into the hood of the thing like joint figureheads on a massive land yacht. It was my method of transportation for years. Before we splurged and bought our second car, all four of us would plow though the autumn leaves or the sludge of spring, the pram at heart of our passage.

All of my babies have ridden in that buggy. All of them have slept in it, out in the backyard at the foot of the stoop, with nothing but the canopy of our broad-leafed elm between their sweet eggshell cheeks and the sloping afternoon sun.

"But, I thought we might fix it." My feeble protest is lost in the scrape and shuffle of the garage door swinging down to block my view of newly ordered garden tools and our six bicycles suspended from the ceiling by their steering posts. Even Will rides now. He begged his dad to take the training wheels off his two-wheeler this spring and now he's as good as the girls.

"We?" He smiles and slaps his leather-gloved hands together again, anxious to get underway. "Come on, the dump closes early on a stat."

It's Thanksgiving Day, deeply autumn, but the snow hasn't come yet and the wooden Adirondack chairs seem to hunker down on the grass, obstinate and reluctant to be stored. The sunlight on their broad arms and deep, low-slung seats makes their primary colours glow, and with my sunflowers only slightly wilted and the hearty heads of marigolds still poking through the ruins of the frost-nipped tomato plants, I can almost imagine August.

"Jeannie. Jeannie? Hey, you coming or not?"

"What about the kids?"

"Allison will mind them. I'll tell her we're going."

He swings back into the yard and tramps to the back door, hollering at our eldest daughter, who is half-heartedly practising the piano. As soon as he moves through the door, the tortured music stops. They are consulting, and both appear on the back landing.

Allison is twelve-and-a-half, a tall, slender child totally unaware of her own ponytailed loveliness. She was a serious baby, shy even, and cautious about each new discovery. Shades of that early reticence still linger.

"How long are you going to be gone?"

"Forty-five minutes, an hour, tops."

"Just keep an ear open and half an eye on them, Allie," I say. "Cut up an apple for Will if he squawks. Natalie and Jen are playing ponies so they probably won't even know we're gone."

"I don't feel great."

Tom ignores her. "Oh, come on, Al. You can give the piano a rest and get some fresh air. You guys even have time for the park if you leave right away. "

"The park's for babies. We'll hang here." She smiles reluctantly at her dad.

"Thanks, kiddo," he says, ruffling her hair. "Maybe we'll even bring you back a treat from the dump." He's down the stairs in a second and doesn't see her roll her eyes.

"What's wrong?" I ask. It's the fretting mother voice, not the rough-and-tumble cheer of her daddy. It seems it's the only voice I've got left these days. My mother voice has consumed all the others.

"Oh, nothing." The screen door bangs and she's gone. A trill from base to treble is her flippant farewell to practising. In my mind's eye I watch this rush past the piano and see her flop onto the couch, reaching for her latest book. She's taken to reading my novels — Laurence, Atwood, Drabble — because "they last longer." I shake my head and climb into the car.

"It smells funny in here."

"Roll down your window. We've got a date at the dump."

Tom's in a good mood. He likes order and he's achieved some semblance of that in the garage. The smell proves it. So I roll down my window and settle back in the passenger seat. It's a glorious autumn afternoon and getting out of the city lifts my spirits.

"Did you used to bring things back from the dump?"

"Oh, yeah. My dad was a great picker. I think it was the handyman in him. He'd bring stuff home that someone had tossed because they didn't know how to fix it. Mostly electric gizmos, small fiddly stuff he'd tinker with in the basement."

Tom laughs. "I remember one winter he spent hours rebuilding this appliance that had an electric can opener on one side and an ice crusher on the other. Replaced the motor and everything. He must have gotten his wires crossed somewhere because when my mom went to open a can of soup the whole machine started shaking like crazy. Tomato soup went all over the kitchen. She threw the gadget out in the yard, she was so mad. An ice crusher, imagine. Just what we needed in January."

I do imagine it. I see Tom and his brothers laughing madly while the refurbished appliance dances across the kitchen counter splattering thick red blobs of condensed soup across the frosted windows. I see the father's face, amazed at his agitating creation. And I see the mother on her knees afterwards, dishcloth in hand, cleaning the mess off the cupboard fronts, the fridge, the floor. The dishwater is the colour of blood.

When she opens the back door and heaves the piece of dump junk out the door, I applaud. I imagine its ridiculous weight sinking into a snowbank, disappearing for good. Its removal from the household is not a victory. I feel sorry for Tom's mother, a woman in a household of men.

My husband is a man in a household of women. His father used to bring things home from the dump. My husband takes things there. *My* things.

I cast back to my last baby, and those milky sweet times ease this unreasonable anger.

The twins were both sleeping in the pram the afternoon I found out our fourth and final child was the son we barely dared to hope for after our three daughters were born. I remember feeling slightly guilty looking at them slouched together in the belly of the buggy, all sweat and curls, plump little limbs entwined, exhausted from the fresh air and missed afternoon nap. They had just turned three, and I had barely recovered from their toddler days when William announced his imminent arrival with the all-too-familiar nausea. My obstetrician confirmed the pregnancy and volunteered information about the baby's sex. I decided I might as well know.

That evening Tom told me he guessed the gender right away by the way I tried to hide my pleasure. The grin, my secret knowledge, played on my mouth. I was happy all right, but it seemed a betrayal to the girls, as though somehow they weren't enough and we needed males to bookend our family.

When Will came, we all liked him, of course, but it was Allison who claimed him as her own. The twins were an indisputable unit who allowed an older sister into their play only when it suited them. But Will was wide open and ready to be loved. Allison spent hours playing with him, lugging him around the house, talking to him, dressing him up in her old clothes or the tattered cast-offs from the twins to further disguise his gender.

I let her take him out in the pram and they'd wheel around the block for hours, playing a game called Runaway Baby, where she'd get the buggy up to a certain speed and then let go, running alongside making faces at the unsuspecting passenger until the liberated pushcart came to a wallowing halt on the grassy boulevard. In her own way, she was practising being a mommy and Will was the ideal guinea pig. He loved speed. He embraced danger.

There was something more aggressive about Will right from the start. Clad in a drooping diaper and some wispy floral blouse, he would transform innocent toys into weapons and make combat noises with his pouty, kissable mouth. Block towers would crash to the ground, helicopters were shot from the sky, ships would sink and vehicles were rendered wheelless by the force of their fiery crashes. Will was my war baby.

He was also the one I least wanted to grow up. After Allison taught him how to tie his own shoes, he'd never let me help. He'd push me aside and I'd wait, exasperated, while he concentrated on making those two loops, that complicated cross-under of the bow. It would be so much quicker if he let me do it for him.

"You're pissed off about the pram, aren't you, Jeannie?"

Ah, perceptive Tom. So subtle, so delicate, so new-age sensitive.

"No."

"Yes, you are. I can tell. You've hardly said a word."

"I was thinking about your mom, about the ice crusher."

"Okay." He swallows my lie because he doesn't want a fight. Neither do I, but it's there, anyway. A simmering thing that I can't articulate.

We're on the outskirts of the city now, near the oil refineries. On my side of the highway farmland rolls in fields of yellow and brown. Those swaths that haven't been harvested have been baled. In a distant field there's only stubble on the ground, and just beyond, the next field has been plowed in preparation for spring planting. The farmers are readying for winter, the long season of darkness and dormancy.

Turning toward Tom is like looking into a different picture. His face is framed by giant industrial oil and gas plants, a massive tangle of pipes and stacks connected by lines to huge domed holding tanks. The refineries cluster together, four or five separate complexes belching smoke and steam and flared gas into the winter quickened air. There's no downtime here. Men work shifts at the oil refineries around the clock, seven days a week, fifty-two weeks a year. Tom worked the line for years until he got his ticket and moved up to management. Now he makes sure his guys keep production up, keep feeding the relentless processing system, the hungry maw of the machines.

"What do you want for supper tonight?"

He looks at me, puzzled. "I don't care."

"Well, someone has to care."

I can't believe my battleground is so small and domestic. So impossibly mundane. Tom doesn't take the bait. He's probably sorry he asked me to come.

We have to drive onto a large scale which weighs our car before we arrive at the booth. A man in a blue uniform slides open the little glass window.

"Got any batteries, hazardous household goods, corrosives or tires in there?" he asks.

"Nope. Couple of bicycle tires."

"No problem. It's a ten-dollar minimum per ton. Pay on your way out."

He waves us through the gates and we roll towards a parking lot at the edge of a man-made gully. Tom backs in and we both get out of the car. Below are dumpsters with large mechanical arms attached. The arms crank up and fall every minute and a half, pulverizing the material cast into the dumpster. It's efficient waste management. It's impressive actually, and both of us watch in silence as the heavy crushing arm smashes the items in the dumpster before a mechanical rake drags the garbage out of the way.

"Oh, my."

Tom hands me his gloves and pops the hatch. We grab the garbage and start to throw it over the bank into the jaws of the crusher. I fling an old clothesline and some drywall board covered with chalk drawings by the children. Tom takes the bigger bits, the broken bureau and a rusted lawn chair and heaves them over the side.

The pram, lodged at the back of the station wagon, is awkwardly compressed and we have to grab it on each side and pull the handle down to get it out of the car. We both struggle to get a grip low down and heave together. The force of our release opens it up. The burgundy hood flops open, the compressed carriage spreads and for a moment it is full again, a baby buggy spinning its wheels in mid-air. It hangs suspended, beautiful and terrible, until it thuds to the bottom of the dumpster moments before the heavy arm descends. Although I close my eyes and look away, I hear the scream of metal upon metal and the yielding crunch of the frame. My pram is raked away.

"That'll be ten bucks," says the gatekeeper after our empty vehicle is reweighed and we proceed in silence through the gates.

"Are you okay?"

The empty fields and the setting sun console me and I am able to smile at him wanly as we roll home. Why would he understand? How can I expect it of him? He no more cares for the pram than I care for the refinery. We are worlds apart on the trip home, but at least my unfocused anger has dissipated.

The house is warm, lit from within, when we return. Tom parks the car in the garage with a swollen sense of accomplishment. I hurry in through the back door, anxious to see my children. The twins rush up. "Mom, Mom. It's Allison. Allison needs you." There is excitement, almost panic, in their fluttering bird voices. "She's in the bathroom and she won't come out."

I feel the weight of the day lift off me; my feet become light as adrenaline rushes though my body. I hurry through the kitchen to the darkened hallway. There is a thin crack of light under the door.

"Allison? Allison, honey? Are you okay? Let me in. It's Mommy."

I touch the knob, expecting the door to be locked, but it turns in my hand. "Allison?"

She is sitting on the toilet. Her panties between her knees are stained a rusty burgundy. She looks up at me expectantly. Neither of us speaks.

WITH CHILD

I t is the same grocery store chain but the advertisements in the window boast different items. On this side of town, white bread is on sale for sixty-nine cents. Kraft Dinner, the surreal orange noodles shouting violence from their trademark blue box, are two for ninety-nine. If you buy something called a Sugar Pop, the second one is free.

Paul thinks of the grocery store in his own neighbourhood. Do they even sell white bread? He can visualize a display of imported chocolate next to the coffee beans but he can't imagine a Sugar Pop. Instead he sees a small capsule inserted below the skin, releasing sugar. It's an absurd notion but he knows exactly how it came to him.

He pays her not to reproduce. Sometimes the ethics of this agreement trouble him and snatches of ceremony and incantation from his childhood come back to niggle at his conscience. Most of the time, however, he can file the Catholic guilt pretty quickly, especially when he sees Margaret lumbering towards him.

Today she's wearing a man's jacket, red plaid, frayed around the buttonholes and bottom. It draws attention to her size. The very girth of her is alarming, and he hopes to God there hasn't been an accident, a miscalculation. She looks sloppy and distinctly unwashed, but her smile is genuine. Guileless. She's probably dressed up for this meeting. Or at least dressed. Paul suspects Margaret spends most of her days in a faded blue robe, smoking and watching her soap operas on TV.

"Hi, Dad." *Today Dad. Usually Paul.*

He takes her elbow, deeply dimpled now, and steers her inside Cousins Café, the pre-arranged meeting place. The screen door bangs and a tiny man mindlessly polishing an eight-slice toaster looks up. Paul scowls. *Probably got his delivery of sixty-nine-cent loaves. Throws a couple of pieces in the toaster, smear of margarine across the top and it's toast at a buck-and-a-half a pop. No wonder the poor will always be with us*, he thinks.

"You hungry?" he asks as they slide into a booth, facing each other.

She immediately reaches for smokes. "Can't eat yet," she says. "It's too early. Makes me sick to eat so early. Just coffee." Again, that lovely girl smile. "Thanks, Dad."

"You're okay, aren't you? You're not, you know..." He motions to his stomach, hands juggling the dead air, the unspeakable word.

Margaret laughs. "I'm not what? Knocked up? Isn't that what you used to say?" She lights her cigarette, and inhales deeply as Paul scans the café to see who's heard. "I doubt it. You've seen to that, haven't you?"

And it's true. He not only pays for and oversees the implant, but they've negotiated a monthly allowance, which he threatens to cut off if she has it removed.

Margaret. Margaret and Emily. His girls. His sad, broken, irreparable daughters. Emily is in a home now, sixty miles up the valley. Is she happy? The thought plagues Paul. She seemed happy, last time he saw her. When? Three weekends ago now?

Emily tripping off the bus, gangly legs and arms akimbo, laughing and talking in the speeded-up voice that almost passes for normal. "I did it, Paul. See? See? I told you, told you. And he," she points to the bus driver, "wants to be my boyfriend. Don'tcha? Don'tcha? See, Paul, he does. See him smile like that?" And then in a chant: "I can ride a bus, with my boyfriend, boyfriend," until Paul pulls her to the privacy of the car.

Emily's on a track team now, aiming for a place in the Special Olympics. She's better off there, than here, with him. Or her sister.

"Jay thinks you should give us more money," says Margaret, stirring two teaspoons of sugar into her coffee. "Jay says it ain't right, what you're doing. Now I'm eighteen, Jay says I should be able to decide for myself."

"*Isn't* right, Margaret. Not *ain't* right. And, as you know, I don't particularly care what Jay says."

She narrows her eyes, defensive. "We're going to have a baby, Paul. Jay says if we don't get more money we're going to have a baby. The welfare's a lot more with dependants, Jay says. And you know what, Paul? I don't even care about the money. I want a baby with Jay. I want to, and I'm going to, and you can just screw off. I'm eighteen now and that's old enough."

"Margaret, Margaret,"' he placates, sorry now he brought up the subject. "Don't be like that. I'm your dad, remember? I want what's best for you. Remember? And if it sounds like I don't like Jay, it's just that I think you deserve someone..." Someone brighter? Someone with a three-digit IQ? Someone who could hold a job, who didn't drink and smack Margaret around when the welfare ran out and the rent was due? "...someone who understands you better, that's all."

"He does understand me. Better than you, anyways. He loves me."

Paul can't argue this one. Margaret's ideas of love are deformed, patched-together memories of early childhood mixed up with the mess he and Sarah made of things.

Love. He'd loved Sarah once, or at least he thought he did. He'd loved her so much he'd taken on these children, these girls, in the hopes their adoption would somehow make them the family Sarah craved. It was crazy, really, thinking that bringing two damaged little children into their lives could plug up Sarah's pain.

Paul shudders, remembering. First the succession of false pregnancies, the deflated hope, the rounds of humiliating tests and the inevitable accusations of infertility and failure. In the end it was determined it was she who was unable to conceive. He, with no burning desire to procreate, was fine. Sarah's test revealed internal atrocities, scarred fallopian tubes as a result of endometriosis, and something foreign and sinister, a large uterine fibroid polyp that couldn't be removed without extensive damage to the womb.

She was devastated, of course, and for the longest time refused comfort. Sex was out of the question. And more than his desire for intimacy, it was love for her that made him agree to the adoption.

Did he love the girls when they came? He pitied them, he knows that. Margaret was eight, hunched, spooked and unspeaking, when she arrived. He'd held out more hope for Emily, two years younger, two years less afraid, but her damage was done before her birth and no amount of love could change it. Sarah tried, but it was an uphill battle and gradually, particularly as the girls developed into sullen, disturbed teens, she gave up.

It was by degrees that she left them, an easing away, not the total abandonment of the other, natural mother. Sarah simply found another project. Another man. He was far less troubled than the girls, and, unlike them, he was able to give Sarah back the undying admiration she needed. Before Paul was even aware of trouble in their marriage, it was over. Sarah moved in with the man and left Paul to manage their former life.

• • •

They are in the car heading north from Halifax. It is the summer after Sarah's departure. Paul is still reeling from the separation, hoping she'll come back. The children give his days structure, and for the first time since they arrived, he needs them more than they need him. A few unsuccessful sleepovers at Sarah's new house has made it increasingly clear the burden of their care rests on Paul.

He thinks about sending them back, even goes as far as to call Social Services for information on their natural parents, for Sarah had arranged an open adoption. Paul learns his daughters are from eastern Cape Breton Island, from a small town called Loch Lomond. Their mother's name is Dulsey. Dulsey Prue.

He finds the place on a map, traces the thin red line up and across the causeway at the Straits of Canso until the road forks, the red line continuing north to the picturesque Cabot Trail, and the road to Loch Lomond hitching east, first a grey line to St. Peters and then broken grey, 80 kilometres inland to the Loch. *Dulsey Prue.* Paul whispers the name under his breath as he plans their journey. An outing. Just to see.

Emily is snapping gum loudly in the back seat, occupied with a Barbie doll. Margaret, dubious, stares out the window as farmland gives way to scraggly bush. She is humming something from the radio, from a few miles back, when they could still pick up a signal. She's nervous. Paul wonders how much of this country she remembers.

"We don't have to see anyone, you know," he reminds her gently, touching her leg. "We can just stay overnight and come right back."

"I want to go to the funeral. You promised," pipes up Emily from the back. "I want to see my mother. She'll be there, won't she, Paul? You promised she would."

"Hush, Em. Yes, she'll probably be there. We'll see what happens, okay? Nobody has to do anything they don't want to. Okay, Margaret?" She smiles wanly and continues to gaze at the passing landscape until Emily thrusts her Barbie between the front seats.

"She's bleeding. She's bleeding. She's men-stir-rating. She's having a baby," shouts Emily, waving the Barbie around in a frenzy. She has smeared Margaret's lipstick, bright red, between the doll's legs. Margaret grabs it by its long blonde hair, and before either of them can speak, rolls down the window and flings it out.

"You're so stupid, EmEm," she mutters, arms crossed, staring straight ahead. Emily shrieks. In the rear-view mirror Paul watches the red and flesh-coloured splotch of plastic twisted in the ditch get smaller and smaller.

The funeral is an excuse. The girls' grandfather has died. The social worker called Paul to let him know, and he, contemplating the trip anyway, agrees to take them up there, to pay respects. Unlike Margaret, he does not know what to expect.

Paul calls Dulsey Prue from their motel, anxious to do the right thing.

"Bring 'em home, to here," she says, markedly unenthusiastic. "He's been laid out for a day now, but there's still a few of our people around. We won't bury him till tomorrow when a priest can come up the lake. Ya can bring 'em round home, though. Won't hurt 'em to see, I don't expect. Growed up now, ain't they?"

But because they are still children, only fourteen and twelve, he goes alone on reconnaissance, leaving the girls in the motel with pay-TV, sodas and strict instructions not to go out. Or let anyone in.

The drive around the lake is spectacularly picturesque. The countryside is pristine. There are no billboards. Highway markers are few and signs indicating dwellings are hand-painted. *Eggs*, reads one, and a slab of wood clumsily fashioned into an arrow points down a track towards the lake. The sign at the Prue place reads *No Trespassing*. Paul knows he's in the right place because of the black ribbon tied around the gate post. He turns the Peugeot into the lane.

The house at the bottom of the road is a sprawling, ramshackle affair. Additions are built on additions and sheds attach themselves to the main structure with unpainted plywood, corrugated tin and cinder blocks. The house looks suspiciously like it will collapse in on itself.

A black dog, chained to a steel ring, barks menacingly, announcing Paul's presence. The yard is littered with bits of broken automobiles, tin cans and dog shit. A bundle of faded plastic flowers leers from the grey-green bowl of a discarded toilet, and from behind the house a chainsaw whines.

A woman comes out to the yard, kicks the dog squarely in the ribs and stands before his car, hands on hips. Paul is instantly struck by her resemblance to the girls. As he gets out of the car, Dulsey Prue scowls.

"Yer comin' alone, then?" she asks, ignoring his outstretched hand.

"I thought I'd bring the girls later," he stammers, unable to hide the terrible stab of recognition he feels looking at the face of this woman.

She is old beyond her years but her face is unmistakably the face of Margaret and Emily. She has the same sloped brow beneath a shock of unruly hair. Her eyes are narrow, suspicious, and thin lips hide missing and stained teeth. Her body beneath a flowered shift seems formless, a lump of boneless flesh. There is a pall over this woman, this Dulsey Prue. It is the pall of poverty, alcohol, poor nutrition, and hopelessness. Paul can smell it. He wants to leave. But it is too late. She gestures for him to follow, and together they go inside the house.

A low-ceilinged vestibule crowded with a freezer, dozens of dead plants and stacks of newspapers opens into a dim kitchen where an enormous man lounges against a kitchen table, drinking Coke from a can and smoking.

"This here is Sonny, my brother," says Dulsey. To him: "His name's Paul. He's the fellow who's looking after my girls that went off to the city couple, three, five years ago. 'Member? Folks wanted to 'dopt them away from Daddy and the lot of you? I let 'em go. They was mine, but I let 'em go anyways."

Sonny only grunts and looks briefly at Paul and then back at his sister. "Daddy's dead now, Dulse. Don't you go speaking nothing wrong about the dead, ya hear?" He stubs out his cigarette in a saucer on the table and turns to Paul. "What's a guy like you want with two little girls?" It's an accusation.

"My wife, she couldn't have any girls — children at all, that is — and we, we thought...the city might offer, you know, more opportunities for young girls."

Sonny grunts again. "You want to see Daddy?"

The coffin is laid out in the front room. The bottom half, the unopened portion, is set up as a makeshift bar. Empty beer cans crowd every surface and ashtrays overflow. A thin light penetrates the heavy drapes and plays on the corpse, making it alone look animated. Two people in a darkened corner of the room frown as Paul enters. He has seen the look countless times before on the faces of his daughters. Another person sleeps on a swayback sofa. In the mouth-breathing sleep of the man on the sofa, Paul hears Emily, sees Margaret. They are undeniably, irrefutably linked to this family in a way that they will never be linked to him.

It is worse, somehow, seeing the old man. Not even the waxy white pallor of death can disguise the downturned mouth, the fallen face crushed by broken dreams and daily squalor. Misery is in the poorly pressed shirt with its frayed collar, and anger, too, disguised in the hand set across the chest strangling a rosary in a rough knuckled fist.

Paul looks briefly at the body and turns away, knowing only that his girls, safe in the highway motel, must never look upon this grey dead face, must never set foot in this dim sour place. He turns to leave, but they are standing, all of them, Dulsey and Sonny and the two others, children or siblings or twisted incestuous offspring of this terrible corpse. They block his way.

Sonny speaks, his great ham-hock arms folded. "We'll bury our own, city man. You've got no need poking around here. Them girls could come, like we said, but not you. You're not one of ours."

"No," said Paul. "No, you're right, I'm not." *And neither are they anymore*, he thinks. "I'm sorry I bothered you." He slides by, escaping to the open air.

The girls never meet their mother. He buys Emily an ice cream float in the gas station to stop her tears and they go back. An hour outside the city, in the gathering shadows, Margaret confesses: "I thought you were going to leave us there. With them." And he protests loudly to quell his guilt, and feels her head against his shoulder, trusting and heavy with sleep.

• • •

The child comes almost nine months to the day after Paul and Margaret's meeting in Cousins Café. Jay's departure had been earlier in the year, when Margaret was five months gone. When Paul goes to visit Margaret and the baby, two days after she's come home from the hospital, Margaret answers the door in her blue robe. The television is on without sound. Her hair is combed and, while she looks tired, there is something about her face Paul has not noticed before. "He's sleeping," she says, awkwardly accepting the flowers he's brought and leading him to the cradle. Paul peers into the blue and white layette with trepidation. But the baby is perfect. He lies on his back, blissfully unaware of scrutiny. His large head is crowned with shocking black hair and his features are regular and lovely. His lips move in his sleep, sucking, and a tiny bubble forms and breaks on his perfect mouth.

"He looks like you, Paul," teases Margaret, scooping her sleeping child to her breast with instinctual tenderness.

"Yes," whispers Paul, unable to take his eyes off the two of them, standing in the glow of the voiceless television. His voice and chest constrict, as he is flooded with something pure and sharp, almost painful. "Yes, he does, Margaret," he whispers. "He looks like me."

HARMONY

When they first move into the sinking house, Rose places the blue glass plate in the narrow kitchen window where it catches the morning sun. It balances on the centre sash and hides part of a nasty fracture that runs up the windowpane, splitting near the top into a fragmented spider web. The plate against the cracked glass reminds Rose of an all-seeing eye in a weathered face. It makes her happy, the same way the sunrise and her daughter's sleeping face make her happy.

The house is poor and uneven. Its foundation has been cracked by too many winters, and when the rental agent showed her the house, Rose immediately thought of a crooked old woman in a wheelchair, slouched in a hallway, waiting for something better. Its history is all that remains.

Rose doesn't particularly like the house, but it is what they can afford and it seems better after Alice dubs it The Sinking House and their laughter seals it snugly from the inside.

They decorate together in an attempt to coax the house into a home. Rose's colourful quilts help. They hide the sofa, tattered and stained with age and Alice's contributions: marking pens without caps, raspberry jam hands and garden muck tracked in on shoes. Rose's other furniture, mostly wicker and wood, settles into its respective rooms and the walls are warmed with books and photographs. The twelve sacred eagle feathers and Rose's collection of mismatched porcelain birds nest together on the craggy slopes of a slanting bookcase.

Still, at night, when they lie together in the big bed, Rose thinks she hears the house groaning. *It needs something,* she thinks, and she sleeps a troubled sleep not knowing what else she can do with their home.

• • •

The day the man comes to inquire about buying the blue plate in the window, Rose is not surprised. It has drawn him in, of course, but the real reason for his arrival has nothing to do with the plate. Rose knows he's a messenger.

"It's just a reproduction," she tells him, when he comes, expressing his desire to buy the plate. "It was only $5.99 at Value Mart. Who knows, they still might have plates like this for sale."

Rose is holding him on the sagging porch, blocking the door to the house with her body. His aura is a deep maroon, dark, too dark, almost mahogany. He's trying to peer around her, to see inside. He extends his hand and it floats before Rose like a foreign and unidentifiable object.

"Name's Emery. Emery Barnes, I got a little collectibles shop in town. *Emery's Antique Barn.* Get it?"

Rose shakes her head but the man continues, speaking without pause.

"This was the Bibby place. They lived here all my life. 'Course Mr. Bibby died some time ago, but Mrs. Bibby just moved up to the Home a short piece back."

When Rose doesn't say anything, he narrows his eyes at her and smiles, showing small rodent teeth before he drops his voice to a conspirator's tone. "I got a lot of their stuff dirt cheap because they didn't know the worth of it. Dirt cheap and good stuff, too. Old stuff. Antiques, a lot of it. I didn't get the piano, mind, but I might yet have a chance for her. Auction coming up next week. Mrs. Bibby taught the children piano. Taught my sisters, taught most kids in town. Not me though. Couldn't get me near the thing. 'Cept now. Love to get near it now."

"Auction?" She can't help herself. She's interested, not so much in what he has said, but why he told her. It shouldn't surprise her anymore. People always tell her things. She is a receptacle of longings and confessions. It has always been like that. But this information about the house, so soon after she'd wondered, has to be an omen.

"Big pieces, farm machinery, balers and combines in the morning, furniture and household lots in the afternoon," says the antique man, eyes casting about, trying to see around her. "Maybe you could get yourself something nice for around this place. Wife makes doilies, sells them at all the gatherings." Emery Barnes thrusts his face so close to Rose, she can smell the luncheon meat on his breath. "Give you a special price, being new around here and all."

"Thank you," says Rose, smiling as Emery Barnes' maroon aura lightens to pink around the edges. "That's very kind."

"You come down to the shop and see me sometime and I'll show you the Bibby pieces. Right nice, most of them."

"Yes," says Rose. "Thank you."

He goes, and Rose shuts the door firmly, feeling as though she's protected the house from something. It's been stripped and that man was involved in the stripping. Stripped. Rose thinks of someone left cold and shivering in a concrete room or forced to take off their clothes in a sweating bar full of red-faced men. Stripped. It's an ugly word and Rose tries not to let ugly words occupy her head. There is enough ugliness in the world without having it live inside her head.

Alice comes downstairs then, looking for lunch, and as Rose watches her daughter dart between fridge and counter, she suddenly realizes what it is the house needs.

"Alice," she says, sitting down and drawing the gangly child onto her ample lap, "we should get a piano." It's spoken as though it is as simple as buying cabbages or potatoes or something hearty to see them through the winter when cheques are farthest apart, but her daughter's narrow face lights up, and Rose is convinced she has hit upon the right thing. Hasn't the blue plate, always a harbinger of truth, told her? And now here is Alice, playing imaginary scales between the lunch crumbs of honey toast. Surely, a double sign. They will get the piano back. They will win the piano at the auction and bring music back into the sad, stripped house.

All week she thinks of it, imagining the woman, Mrs. Bibby, youthful again, sitting upright at the bench beside a small, still child. Notes of such clarity and generosity sound in the room that Rose's eyes tear just thinking about it. They will have the piano and Alice will learn to play.

Sitting at the table that evening, Rose files her unpaid bills in a thick manila envelope while Alice practises her letters in the exercise book sent home from school. With her tongue slightly protruding and her head bent over the scribbler, the child is a study in concentration. Rose sees her fingers, thin and long, gripping the pencil, and wishes her daughter the freedom of the keyboard rather than the cramped space where *b*s and *d*s mix themselves up between the strict lines on the page.

• • •

The day of the auction is clear and cold, and Alice insists on finding her winter coat. Her legs protrude like thin stick legs below the bulk of the down jacket and Rose wonders at her remarkable fortitude. They walk to town, to the only hotel, to get instructions. There is a woman behind the desk, filing nails long and curved, painted red.

"Cold enough for you?" she says, as they swing through the doors into the blast of heat. And before they can answer, "And what can I do for youse two pretty little things?" To Alice: "Ain't you something, bundled up like that? What's your name, honey?"

And because Alice has never been shy she licks her lips, ignores the question and asks: "Do you have a car? My mom and I are going to get a piano but we have to walk and I don't want to. I want to get the piano, I mean, because I'm going to play it." She holds up her hands still inside the red mittens as a quick demonstration of unleashed ability. "We always walk everywhere, but it's too cold to walk so far today, even if it is for a piano, but it would be okay if we could go in a car. Maybe you have a car?"

Rose smiles at Alice, amazed to have produced such a child. She really wants to play piano. Imagine, this skittish colt of a girl, a pianist. It must be in her genes. Her father played bass guitar in a band. Or was it lead guitar? Regardless, he was certainly a musician. That part she remembers.

Alice's voice is pitched high, and Rose, who has barely heard the words, imagines them as small shapes, wayward birds dodging the desk clerk's bright talons. The woman speaks again, this time to Rose, and the room comes back into focus.

"...only a quarter of a mile north of here. You'll see the signs. They'd be hard to miss. They're everywhere." She picks up her nail file again and points with it toward the door. Her hand is waving down, up, across. Of course, she's a conductor. The signs are everywhere. Alice tugs her hand and as the piano solo starts, dainty and high in her head, Rose smiles again, bows slightly. "Thank you, thank you. We'll find it, I'm sure. It's waiting for us, you see." And they leave.

Alice pulls her mother back onto the drab ribbed road that winds through empty fields and they walk in a direction that has to be, must be, north.

The first sign is at a crossroads, a plywood board propped up against a yield sign with a pointing arrow and the words AUCTION TODAY spray-painted in Day-Glo green. They trudge on, following the signs to a clump of willows which flanks a rutted driveway. As they turn down the lane, startled birds fly panicked from a clump of trees and disappear up into the winter sun.

"This is it, Mom. This is where it is."

Alice is excited now. She dances down the drive, her cheeks flushed with walking and cold and the excitement of the instrument Rose has woven into her bedtime stories, the piano that has sneaked into her dreams and sounded with the sweet clear notes of ownership and possession.

The auction is in a barn. There are people outside, men mostly, surveying farm equipment or pawing through lots of gardening tools and paint tins and fertilizers. They run their hands along the underbelly of tin troughs still encrusted in the joins with bits of mud and straw, and they stroke the shanks of hoes as if to measure their worth.

A few of the men look at Rose and Alice as they walk into the yard. Most don't, and Rose is glad when they are swallowed by the dim barn. Inside, Alice pulls closer to her mother.

"Let's find it," she whispers in the sweet hay-smelling gloom. "Let's find our piano." And they make their way towards the back of the barn where the big household items stand patient and dumb.

At the front of the barn the auctioneer has started his pitch. Groups of women press around him as he moves his soapbox between the lots. His voice is bad music, three or maybe four sour notes sounding again and again in rapid succession. It's a dull drone behind them.

Alice stops. In front of them is the piano. It's an upright, a solid wooden box, cherry-coloured, with delicately curved legs supporting the keyboard. The pedals are dulled brass, the bench has the lustre of wood well-worn. The piano seems suffused with a soft golden-red light. They stand before it without speaking until Alice touches one of the small knobs and gingerly lifts the lid to reveal the keyboard. The wood folds in on itself, and the yellowed ivory keys smile their gap-toothed grin. *It's glad*, thinks Rose. *The piano knows we will bring it home.*

Reverently, Alice strikes a note in the low register but, at the same time it sounds, the auctioneer's voice rings out *Sold,* and the note is lost, its resonance echoing in the word. Rose and Alice look at each other, eyes gleaming with anticipation. *Yes, yes,* their eyes say. *Another sure sign.*

The group of bidders is moving closer, stationed now by a cherry highboy. The words of the auctioneer, strung together, are wrapping the bidders in a taut net. Two women are bidding on this piece. A stout, older woman with a tight perm is challenged by a younger woman, slicker and even more polished than the hotel clerk. The auctioneer is playing them off each other, back and forth, back and forth, until one voice remains. Rose closes her eyes, steadies herself against the great giving weight of the piano. She hopes the older woman has won the bidding. Hers was a more genuine desire, her voice had the need. But no, she has been silenced. The other, the woman who now runs a proprietor's hand across the furniture, will take this and sell it in the city. She is a dealer. Rose feels suddenly afraid for the piano. She is afraid this slick dealer will take away their piano.

The crowd surges forward, and the auctioneer stoops to move his box in front of the piano. Rose is pressed back against the instrument. Alice ducks underneath and crouches by the pedals, sheltered from the throng.

"This beautiful oak upright was made in Germany in the last half of last century, folks, and if I'm not wrong — which I'm usually not — it was brought to our fair province on the backs of oxen. Yes, oxen. Your ancestors, ladies and gentlemen, wanted music in their lives and wanted it enough to fetch this exquisite piano from the old country. It's a rare piece, an unusual piece, a unique piece of furniture that would make any homeowner proud. If you'd like to have this beautiful piano in your living or dining room…think of the tinkling ivories, friends, think of the joy this beauty would bring to old and young alike.

"Do-I-hear-twelve-hundred-dollars?-Or-if-not-gimme-a-cool-thousand-I-got-a-thousand-Will-I-hear-eleven-hundred?-A-thousand-a-thousand-yup-and-eleven-hundred!-Eleven-hundred-we-got-eleven-hundred-Do-I-hear-twelve?-Twelve-twelve-it-ain't-too much-to-ask-for-culture-folks…"

Rose reaches into her pocket and feels the few crumpled bills, and beneath them the heavy weight of coins. She looks down between her legs and there is her daughter's face, a pale moon clouded in anxiety. *What price music?* she thinks. *What price happiness?* And she pulls her hand from her pocket and thrusts it up, holding it above the head of the dealer lady, above the heads of all the other people, up to the rafters, up beyond the roof of the barn, up, up to where white birds fly towards the sun. Rose holds her hand steady and straight and reaching up until the word *Sold* falls down upon her ears like a perfect note. And in that one moment, in the moment of silence that follows, while the group shuffles on to the next piece, the piano truly belongs to them.

THE ACCIDENT

It should have been about her. You'd think it would be. After all, it was her front end crushed, her body flung forward, her world sandwiched between a steering wheel and a seatbelt. But it wasn't about her at all. It was about everybody else.

Let's take a look at the most distant players. For her husband, the accident is extremely inconvenient. The first thing it does is take him away from a much anticipated business meeting that is to culminate in a five-star restaurant.

A security guard comes into the room. All heads swivel in unison at this unusual interruption. After the guard stoops and whispers discreetly in his ear, there is an awkward pause. He has to tell his colleagues something. The potential client, Mr. Winters, has a brow like a snowplow and his boss looks both annoyed and concerned. "My wife, it seems, has been in a traffic accident." No, he knows nothing else. Will they excuse him, please? He must find a telephone.

The room, when he leaves, is buzzing, and he wonders briefly how his proposal, now forgotten and likely to languish for weeks, could bring the same energy into a room of stuffed suits.

The security guard who has brought the news now carries himself with the stature of someone in the know, the unfortunate but necessary bearer of bad tidings. As they leave the room the husband appraises him. He is young and the shoulders of his coat are too big. What would he do if there were a real problem, a drunken madman, say, or someone with a pistol and a grudge? The security guard is just a kid. He's scrawny. The collar of his starched white shirt barely touches the skin on his neck, which (oh, why did he look!) is pimply and raw. He walks tall, however. Perhaps he'll flesh out someday. This has been an important moment in his chosen career.

In fact, bringing the news of the accident is the very reason the security guard wears the uniform. Now he knows. Checking empty hallways and marking burned-out light bulbs pale in comparison to this mission of mercy. He wonders how the man is taking the news of his wife's accident. He wonders if it is serious and if the businessman loves this woman who, this very moment, may be lying in a ditch or may be strapped to an ambulance gurney. If it's a homicide (how deliciously gruesome that word feels in his mouth) what will this businessman do?

The security guard thinks briefly of the girl, Tami, the sweet young secretary who called so panic-stricken she'd forgotten to give him the name of the man's company. The security guard himself had to call back, and explain gravely that their conference rooms were booked by company not personal names and, if it were indeed urgent, perhaps he should have more details?

And what of Tami, she of the quavering voice? Imagine what this has done to her phone manner, she who almost always chatted with the wife before putting her through. This event has both shattered and raised her confidence. After the voice on the other end of the line — the voice which for the first time she didn't recognize — squeaked out the news of her circumstances, suddenly everyone wanted to go to lunch with Tami to hear what had happened and what she knew and who it was that had called her back. She was congratulated on staying calm and exclaimed over for forward thinking: what a good idea it was to locate the boss at his meeting via the security company. A husband needs to know these things, the sooner the better.

Tami wonders momentarily if she'll be given a promotion; move out of reception to take over fat Lola's job of invoicing or perhaps even Selina's job in personnel, but she dismisses that idea when she thinks about the wife. What if she were really hurt? Her boss could be distracted for weeks, months even. Tears well in Tami's eyes, because, let's face it, this morning has been traumatic and maybe she'll just slip out early, seeing as the boss won't be back anytime soon. She saw a sweater at Gap that might look good with her new black miniskirt.

Had enough of the bit players? We'll go briefly back to the husband now, just to check his condition. Oh, dear. He's not only a little embarrassed about the circumstances, he's angry too. At his wife's office, where she bloody well should be at this hour, the telephone rings and rings. He can smell the wood-fired grill and the filet mignon. He imagines a balsamic reduction and root vegetables pan-fried in garlic and vermouth. He can almost taste the Merlot. His wife has been in a car accident. He'll call his office. Tami will know and, of course, she tells all, even tearing up once or twice in the account. How typical, he thinks. His wife calls, drops a bombshell with little or no other information, and then hangs up.

Still, he's relieved. She's called. It couldn't be too bad if she's called. And even though Tami said she sounded strange, that's likely more to do with worry than hurt. She probably *is* worried, too, about smucking up the car. Rightly so, he thinks. Their premiums will go up for sure, now. He'll go for lunch, try to talk his way back into the proposal and call in an hour. He's feeling a bit guilty about the lunch but it's noon, and a guy's got to eat, hasn't he? He looks at his watch. He'll call at 1:00. There's usually a lull between the entrée and the dessert. He hopes it won't be crème caramel. Why do high-end restaurants think lumpy pudding with a crust makes a classy dessert? He looks up and down the hall to make sure the pimply security guard has gone back to his snooze duties at the front desk, straightens his tie and heads to the dining room.

Now we'll zoom in closer to the accident. Who is taking centre stage? Shouldn't it be the hapless victim, the woman (until now simply referred to as "the wife") who rammed her little tin box of a Japanese compact into the blank white wall of an illegally left-turning Volvo? Why no, it's not her at all. It's the witness, a stout woman with a very red face. You can tell she is used to being in charge. And she *is* in charge. She's demanding a cellphone. She's punching in 9-1-1. No one can stop her. She is a steamroller. She saw everything, the little blue car tooling down the road, the big white Volvo station wagon turning in front, against the green light. She wanted to cry out, hadn't the time, and now, would you look at this mess! There she was, minding her own business, just dropping little Caylie off at playschool so she could go see Mitchell's teacher and find out why he isn't getting better grades and, wouldn't you know it, some fool rushes in, trying to cross a lane of traffic.

The lady in the blue car is hurt. There's no question. She needs an ambulance. She's wandering around looking dazed and disoriented. Where the hell are the goddamn cops when you need them? She punches new numbers into the cellphone and demands an officer. You can't help but hear her voice, loud and demanding:

"Yes, both vehicles can be driven and are off the road." Pause. "Well, it depends on what you mean by hurt. I think she's in shock." And then, even louder. "Look, officer, I'm just doing my civic duty. You have no right to speak to me like that!" The witness is getting madder and madder. Her blood pressure is rising. She's mad that the cops won't come. They're probably at Tim Horton's. She's mad that they won't send an ambulance despite the fact that she saw the horrendous impact and both cars are likely write-offs, and mostly she's mad at the ridiculously calm voice on the other end of the line, the man who isn't her, on-site, who isn't surrounded by broken bits of glass, who didn't see a damned thing. How dare he question her authority? How dare he? Who does he think he is? She saw it all.

"Give me your superior," she rallies, undaunted, redder than an apple, redder that the reddest beetroot. "You haven't heard the last of this." And then the phone is buzzing in her hand and it seems like her head might separate from her body at that very moment, and it would too, if she weren't so desperately needed by those poor stupid people, not even smart enough to drive. The witness is incensed. We have not heard the last of her, either. Her blood pressure is sky-high.

Her kids will get yelled at. Mitchell's teacher, a young cringing thing in her first assignment, will take it in the neck this afternoon and it's all because someone was in the right place at the right time, because some good citizen witnessed a car accident.

The driver of the white Volvo, the one who obviously caused the accident, is standing at the side of the road, wringing her hands. She's an elderly woman, maybe sixty-eight or seventy, maybe older. She is wringing her hands and muttering. If you listen closely, if you can block out even a little of the witness's roar, you'll hear: "I'm sorry, I'm so, so sorry. Are you okay? Are you hurt? Oh, I'm so sorry." The old lady has a pink scalp beneath the finest cloud of white hair and a ghastly white, white face. She has caused this collision. Of that, there is no question. The passenger side of her white Volvo is crumpled. It looks like tissue paper, scrunched up and discarded. The frame looks twisted, steel shrieks of structural damage, white paint and bits of blue have flaked and fallen and there is glass and the broken orange plastic bits of a turn signal in the rubble. The pale Volvo driver twists her hands together, eyes wide and ingenuous. "I'm so, so sorry," she keeps on repeating.

The red woman holds her anger, the white woman holds her dismay, the other woman, the blue woman, the one in the blue car, the wife, holds on to reality. Barely. All she can think of is reassurance.

"I'm fine," she says, or thinks she says. But is she fine? Hers is an automatic response to the poor, white-faced, hand-wringing woman. She needs to know all is well, and words must be mustered to alleviate that awful fear in the elderly woman's anxious and clouded eyes. But where are her words? Where have they gone? Only a croak comes from the victim's closed throat. She has seen the passenger door of the white Volvo. She has yet to see the front end of her own car. She does not remember crawling out the driver's window. All she can see is the white door that is no longer a door. It has been obliterated. Had there been a child in that seat... But, no, it is too horrible to imagine and her hand floats up to her mouth, smothering the croaking groan. "Thank God you were alone." Her eyes appeal to the old woman. And because she thinks of her only small son, often hurriedly strapped into the front seat, flying through the windshield, she cries out again.

It is not weeping, the sound we hear from the woman-who-has-just-been-in-an-accident. It is not sobbing. It is a cry of agony and gratitude for what might have been but is not. It is shock and hysteria locked in a strange coupling with the need to comfort the older woman and gather into her arms the child who is not even there, to feel his firm flesh against her shaken and bruised body.

There is much more that happens to the blue woman after that initial cry, of course. The requisite papers are exchanged, the witness shouts vivid red instructions and eventually the cars limp off to their respective destinations. Much of what happens afterwards is internal, the feeling of dread and guilt that can't be seen and the more suspicious silent goings-on beneath the skin and, more particularly, the skull of two rattled, battered people.

On the way to the police station to file a report, the black-and-blue woman from the accident goes the wrong way down a one-way street. Her mind registers the mistake just in time, and with a slipstream maneuver she manages to make it safely out of the way of oncoming traffic.

At the police station she doesn't tell of this minor traffic mishap, only what she thinks happened earlier. She talks a lot (too much, she's sure, but she cannot stop) about the sunshine, not that it was in her eyes, because it wasn't, but just how beautiful the day was and how it felt like such a shame to be going to work in an office on such a sunny day, and how she loved the way the sun made the snow blue-white, like the hair of the Volvo driver. She mentions the radio station she was tuned to — CBC One — and its broadcast documentary on home care, but she hastens to add how she'd only been half listening because for her it was too late, her mother had died in a home months before. She was driving, mindful of the road, the green light in front of her, when, with no warning and no possibility of avoidance, the white wall of steel, the Volvo, had turned in front of her. Across one lane, and then hers, but what could she do?

Speed? Oh, likely the speed limit. Perhaps a titch faster, because one does, doesn't one?

Seatbelt with shoulder strap? Of course.

And then? And then, the sickening thunk of metal on metal and her morning coffee cup flying off the dash, breaking the plastic cup holder, and her briefcase and papers spilling over into the front seat, the jerk and lurch of her body, the sharp tug of the seatbelt and, most of all, the sheer amazement that this could happen on a clear day beneath a still-glowing green light.

"Did you hit your head?" It's the policeman now, looking at her strangely, and she realizes her words haven't quite come out as she'd formed them in her mind. He'd like to send her to see someone medical, right now, but the door has roared open and the wild, red-faced witness is in the shop, set on seeing her complaint realized right here and now, goddamnit. Words now fly over the counter: "I was just trying to help… Treated me like shit… Don't talk to me that way, young man!" And on and on until the victim of the car crash sways out the door, looking pale and bemused.

She must be okay, registers the cop, leaving with that little benevolent smile on her face.

In the privacy of her broken car, whose front door had to be pried open with a crowbar by the lovely young policeman who, right now, is having his ear chewed off by the witness, the pain begins. It starts slowly at first and builds all day until her body is one large throbbing ache and her mind a thrumming, scrambled mishmash of mispronounced words and jumbled sentences, and names that she should know, gone, just gone.

The husband comes to her office eventually, and takes her away, dropping her off outside the clinic. He goes home then, because someone has to be there when the boy gets home from school. He orders two small pizzas — one ham and pineapple, one anchovies and onions and black olives — on his cellphone on the way home and never once suspects his wife is more than just shaken up.

In the aftermath of the accident, Tami gets a two-week respite. The day before her time off begins, the security guard calls up and asks if she'd like to meet for a drink. He'll go in uniform. She'll wear the new pink Gap sweater, the one purchased on "the day."

The old lady, the pale perpetrator, never does discover the outcome of her accident. Her husband, a war vet, handles all the dirty business: the insurance claim, the liability, the letters from the solicitor and, eventually, the inquest. He overhears his wife telling bridge friends, "She was the nicest lady I've ever hit."

The witness, who reads the obits every day, notices the picture and shakes her head. They should have listened. She was the one who saw everything, wasn't she? She tried to help, tried to do her civic duty, but would any of them listen? As she butters her third piece of toast, the witness weighs the possibility of filing a class action suit against the city police.

The husband? Well, here it is only fair to say the husband is deeply grieved and rightly remorseful. To him, it never seemed like more than a fender bender. He wishes he had bought her a better car. He does not remarry for two-and-a-half years, and only then, he tells himself, because the little boy needs a mommy. A child needs a mommy. And so, a brief revision is necessary. In the end, when all is said and done, the accident really was about her, after all.

THE CROSSING

We're taking him home. The others, Mom, Justine and Rob, flew back, but because we need to get Rob's truck back, we're driving.

My oldest brother Rob was already in university when it happened, so he came right away. And Justine, too, being older, didn't leave Mom's side. We watched from the tarmac, the three of us mute as they helped her onto the plane, Justine and Rob, one on each side, for support.

Gord is the first to speak once the rush of the engines has faded and the plane looks small and fake in the sky. "Okay. That settles it. Let's go." He punches Don lightly on the shoulder, looks at me. "You ready?" I nod.

Gord goes around to the driver's side. Don opens the passenger door. It's a bench seat, but still it's going to be cramped. I slide over so the stick presses into my thigh. Don's big now. He stashes some gear behind the seat, hauls the door closed. Gord jiggles the stick in neutral, getting a feel for the truck. It's got a ball, worn smooth, the marking of the gears barely visible. He turns the key and the old green Chev turns over. When did my brothers start taking up so much space?

It shouldn't, but it feels a little bit like an adventure, a thousand-mile road trip straight north. None of us have been there for a long time. We're going home, all three of us, back to the place that formed us, shaped us, and eventually spat us out when it became increasingly clear we weren't settling for the hard rock mining or the soft civil service or the raw wild life of trapline and trade. I felt the stirring in me, the excitement of the travel. I traced it out in my mind as we headed west. Edmonton, Peace River, Manning, High Level, Indian Cabins, Enterprise, and then the Great Lake. Fort Providence, over to Rae, those last seventy miles, Sammy's Beach and home.

The first green highway sign on the swing north kind of pulls me down a notch or two. Yellowknife 1505 km. Yup, it's a trip all right.

Don's tinkering with the radio. Gord is looking straight ahead. It's really close in the cab. It smells like grease and wood shavings and unwashed socks. The box is behind the seat. Dad. He's the fourth passenger. He's the reason for our trip.

How many times had he taken us out and brought us home? Gripping the steering wheel, he drove: Yellowknife, Fort Providence, Enterprise, Indian Cabins, High Level, Manning, Peace River and then The City. A two-week vacation and back again: from Edmonton north; the great Peace valley and that green girder bridge in the centre of town; the moose at Manning; mud in High Level, always mud; a cinnamon bun at Indian Cabins; gas in Enterprise, a ferry schedule and highway reports in Fort Prov; across the mighty Mackenzie and around Great Slave, like circumnavigating an ocean, to home. How many times? I can't count them.

The divided highway ends at Gunn, and the farming fields peter out an hour further north just past Whitecourt. There's nothing but bush between us and the end of this road, nothing but bush and, farther up, bedrock.

"Rob did a good job," says Don. "I felt like he said it best." Gord only nods.

"I liked the Shakespeare."

"What's it from, that quote?"

"It's *Romeo and Juliet*, just after the balcony scene." I'm remembering the movie, not the Complete Works, but I'm not going to tell my brothers that.

Don snorts, laughing: "*Romeo and Juliet?* You gotta be joking. Dad, Romeo? That's the funniest thing I've heard since…"

"Shut up."

Gord doesn't say it loudly, but it's enough to startle us. We both look over at him. The big stupid grin on Don's face dissolves. Gord is crying. He's looking straight ahead at the road and big tears are running down his face and dripping, plop, plop, onto his lap and the steering wheel.

"Sorry, man."

Gord still won't look at us but he doesn't try to stop crying either. He speaks slowly: "*When I shall die, take him and cut him out in little stars, and he will make the face of heaven so fine that all the world will be in love with night, and pay no worship to the garish sun.*" He has memorized it from the eulogy.

"Do you want me to drive?"

Gord nods. He checks the rear-view mirror. He slows, gears down, and pulls the truck over towards the shoulder. When we're stopped and the truck is idling in neutral he turns and looks at both of us. His voice is flat. "He was, you know. He was better than the fucking sun." His face screws up and he puts his head down on his arm, laid across the steering wheel. His back shudders, once, twice, and a strangled sob escapes.

Don nudges me and I put my arm across my older brother's shoulders. My throat hurts again and the tears are welling up in my own eyes. "Yeah, I know. He was. He was, Gord. We were lucky."

Don cracks his door. I feel the cold and the space open up. I'm still sitting really close to Gord. He's been like a brick through the whole thing. He did a lot of the lousy jobs — picked the casket, tipped the mortuary guys, wrote the obit, even ran out to the airport a few times to pick up stray relatives. He was strong, stone-faced, dry-eyed. He was the one who suggested we drive, even went so far as taking the truck in for an oil change between the funeral and the reception. Gord. Now he's bawling, memorizing Shakespeare, just barely hanging on.

Don opens the door on Gord's side. "Come on, pal. You ride."

My brother lifts his head at last and swings his legs around slowly like an old man. He stands up and they are face to face. Don puts his arms out and they embrace briefly, patting each other on the back, the same way you'd pat a baby thrust into your arms by someone you hardly knew. I watch them and then look straight ahead, pretending I didn't see the tenderness. There's nothing ahead of us but blacktop but it doesn't look right. The yellow lines aren't straight, the surface of the road is off-kilter, wonky. Even the afternoon sky is wrong. It's got a strange cast to it, like some primary kid painted it blue and then tried to erase most of it with a pencil eraser. The black streaks are smudges, not clouds.

Cut him out.

As the truck pulls out again and Gord leans his head against the passenger side window, I think of what they cut out. First his chest was opened. They must have had to separate the rib cage to get a good look at the heart. They cut a little bit off it, I think. Or maybe they sewed something up. It was supposed to be simple procedure. No big deal. He sent me a letter. I got it the morning I left. The mailman handed it to me along with a flyer for gumboots and rain gear and a power bill. It sort of slid out from between them and my own heart did a weird flip below my ribcage. This surge of hope like nothing I've ever felt before flooded my whole body when I saw the slanted letters, his distinctive handwriting. *I'll be out of here in no time, Nikki. And, with the food they're giving me, I imagine I'll be fifteen pounds lighter. Imagine that, little rascal, fifteen pounds!* But the date was there across the top, black and white, and what had happened had still happened.

Then my cab was there and my landlady was shaking her head and sort of hugging me, saying *Don't worry, don't worry.* She didn't know about the fifteen pounds or the little rascal or any of that. She just helped me with my stuff and waved me off.

The letter is in my bag. It's proof that he didn't mean to die, he didn't expect to, that they cut him up wrong and something wouldn't go back together and it just got crazy and out of control and what was never supposed to happen, did, and he died. Boom, just like that. One minute you're complaining about the food, the next minute your kidneys have quit and the vital organs are shutting down and nobody knows what to do because it isn't supposed to happen like this.

I haven't shown the boys the letter. I don't know if I will.

"You want to stop for something to eat?" Gord looks better now, like the crying helped lift a couple of those bricks off his chest. He's hungry.

"We can't stop every half hour, guys," says Don. "We've got to get some miles on first. I'll make Valleyview and we'll hit the Husky for gas and grub. How 'bout that?"

"Fine." I say it for both of us because Gord is feeling bad about the crying, I can tell.

It's getting dark and the highway signs keep on reminding us we're in moose country. Every fifty kilometres or so they have a sign shaped like a moose, big rack of antlers, head down, looking like it could stop a semi. The signs are painted in reflective paint that picks up the glare from the headlights, a glowing reminder that we're outside our territory, that this country belongs to someone else.

In the twilight we see three little white crosses in the ditch. One of them has a wreath of plastic flowers on it.

"Must have hit a moose," says Don.

"Or a Moose Crossing sign," says Gord, laughing.

I crane my neck and look over my shoulder out the back window. I can barely see them, but for some reason the crosses make me feel better. Like someone else knows about this sort of thing. Like we three aren't the only ones.

There's hardly any traffic. Some long haulers slow us down a bit when we get stuck behind them but they tend to move to the shoulder if they're fully loaded. Don waves as we pass, saluting the small kindness of the driver. He must have copied that from Dad. It seems like such a grown-up thing to do. But we're not kids anymore, I have to remind myself. I'm twenty-two, Gord's twenty-three and Don will be twenty-one in the fall. I wonder if he'll get his watch. The thought chokes me. I close my eyes and put my head back. Dad bought us each a watch, a good watch, a keeper watch, when we turned twenty-one. It was meant to signify coming of age or something. I used to think it was a hokey idea but now I'm glad.

A watch, ticking away time.

"Been watching the playoffs?" says Don, looking across me to Gord.

"The Leafs look really bad this year."

"But you gotta love the Habs. I think Montreal's going to take the cup this year. Hope so anyway." It's the same banter from our childhood. The same stupid alliances. *I want to be the blue team, you be red.* I can hear Gord's high-pitched voice and I can see both of them lying on their bellies in front of a rectangle of white metal, maneuvering pivotal tin men on metal rods. *He shoots! He scores!* They do the sound effects and the announcer's voice all at the same time. There're books of hockey cards, pored over on weekends and a game of road hockey almost every day after school. We congregate, neighbourhood children and the occasional teenager, to pass a frozen puck beneath the single street lamp, dragging the nets off to the side whenever anyone from the opposing team hollers *car* in the increasing gloom. My brothers get to pick their players, for they are always on opposing teams. Red, Don. Blue, Gord. Montreal and Toronto, cities as foreign to us as the capitals of Europe we memorize for social studies. Some things never change.

I close my eyes and lean my head back against the seat. Their voices blanket me like a familiar quilt. With the constant of the engine sounding, the warmth of the two big bodies on either side, I drift off into some close cousin of sleep.

I am awakened by the truck stopping. We're at a gas station. I have to pee. I'm surprised how dark it is now. My head feels thick and clogged, like I've been trying to swim, trying to breathe, in a pool of cotton balls, light and insubstantial but at the same time suffocating. Don is talking to the gas jockey. Gord is nowhere to be seen.

"Hey."

"I guess I fell asleep."

"I'll say."

"This Valleyview?" I see no valley, no view to speak of, just slush and grime and the hulking shadows of rigs, their reflectors glowing in our headlights.

"Yup. Gord's inside buying road food."

I nod and pull my coat around me. This is just a pit stop. We have to make more miles. Inside the ladies' room the fluorescent bulb buzzes. I look in the mirror and see my face, creased and puffy. I look old, tired and sad. Mechanically, I smile at my own image. Teeth, yellow. Smile, strained. Why bother? The door on the stall won't close but I'm the only one here so I just leave it. I sit down, close my eyes, and feel the weight of the world in the slouch of my shoulders. And who knows how long it will be until we sleep. All the energy for the trip is sucked away by the sluicing toilet, the dirty truck stop, the real purpose of our journey.

I wash my hands and splash some water on my face. The paper towels are rough and prickly, their disposal basket overflowing. I wad mine up and try a behind-the-back shot. Hitting the rim, the towel bounces in. For some reason this cheers me up more than it should and I push out of the grubby washroom to find Gord juggling a couple of over-nuked sandwiches from hand to hand. The plastic wrap has melted through in some places and it's sticking to the white bread. Puffs of steam escaping from the cello-wrapped sandwiches punctuate the sound that's coming out of my brother's mouth.

"Hot...hot...hot...hotta...hotta —"

"How long did you put them in?" I ask, grabbing drinks from the coolers.

"I don't know. Maybe three minutes."

I give him a long look. "Three minutes?"

"Whatever... You got any cash?"

I pull out Dad's credit card. "We're supposed to use this. Remember?"

"Isn't that cancelled yet?" Gord says, scowling. I kick his boot and glower but the clerk doesn't seem to notice anything amiss, just takes the card, punches in the numbers for the gas and the food, and runs the credit card through his machine. For a fleeting second I think about forging Dad's signature but end up signing my own name. We share the same backward-slanting letters, anyway. The clerk doesn't even glance at the slip. We're off again.

"It's still a good two-and-a-half hours to Peace River," says Don, consulting the map. "We could deke into Grand Prairie and spend the night, or do you guys want to press on?"

"What time is it?" I ask.

"Who's in Grande Prairie?" says Gord at the same moment.

"It's almost 7:30, and Dick Becker lives there. Remember Dick? He used to drive the oil truck for the town?

Scrawny kid. In my grade. I'm sure he'd put us all up. He knows...knew...Dad pretty well. In fact, I think it was Dad who got him the job in the first place, after he dropped out in grade eleven. He moved down south about three years ago. Andrew Guardian told me he's into raising horses."

"Let's keep going," I say. I remember Dick. I remember him drunk out of his mind and still pulling on a forty of rye at a bush party near the gravel pits, what? Five, six years ago? I remember him lurching around the fire, slurring the words to a Jimi Hendrix tune, putting his wiry arms around anyone who looked vaguely female. He and Jackie Dupuis disappeared into the shadows that night. The next year she was toting around Emma in a baby backpack, Dick Becker nowhere to be seen. That's what it was like in the end. That could have been me, I suppose, if I'd stayed. There wasn't much to do but drink and make out and roar around in trucks, from bush party to bush party while the surreal summer sun kept its unblinking eye on us through the night. My father spent more than half his life in that small northern town. We're taking him back to scratch a hole in the poor soil and plant him there. He'll never leave now.

"What's the plan? You know, with the box? With Dad?"

"We're going to scatter his ashes," says Gord.

"Yeah, I figured *that* out, but where?"

"On the golf course. Fifth hole. The one that's got that bog."

"No way!"

"That's what he wanted," says Gord, looking at me sharply. "He told us."

I turn to Don. "Both of you?"

"Yup."

"He must have been kidding!"

"He spent a lot of time on that golf course, Nikki. I think that was the only time he really relaxed." Gord nods.

"But it's so undignified." The golf course. What comes instantly to mind is sand, scraggly stunted jack pines, mosquitoes, a rickety wood slat building perched on stilts on the bedrock, uninsulated, a sort of glorified camp cook shack with a makeshift bar and wooden picnic tables inside a huge screened porch. When we were really small we used to go underneath the building looking for coins in the dark sand. Above us, coming through the cracks of light in the floorboards, were the voices of the men, low and laughing. My dad, telling a story. I can see him now. He really did love it out there. It was like a little kid's clubhouse for grown men. They held a midnight golf tournament once a year. Foursomes walking around in the twilight, trailing bristle mats behind them to erase the mark of their passage on the oiled greens. The ravens kept stealing their golf balls and at 5:00 a.m. they always held a huge pancake breakfast to celebrate the longest day of the year.

"Dad always had trouble on the fifth," says Gord, chuckling.

And suddenly I'm envious. They spent more time with him than I did. They were boys. They golfed with him when they were older. He never showed me how to hold a club, how to swing, how to keep your knees bent and your eye on the soaring ball. He never told me where he wanted his goddamn ashes spread.

It passes over me quickly, this anger, like a twist of paper burning, a flare-up, insubstantial heat, and then nothing. Ashes. I sigh audibly, then focus on the road. A green highway sign flashes by — Peace River 258 kilometres. We'll get in around 9:30 and if we drive through the night we could hit Yellowknife by mid-morning the next day.

Suddenly, more than anything, I want to get there. I want this trip to be over and done with. This is too long, this road. It's bringing back too many memories. My brothers are taking up too much space in this small cramped truck, and they know things I don't know. Maybe we *should* have stopped at Dick Becker's. Maybe he could have told me some things about Dad, too. Some things I didn't know. *Your Dad believed in reincarnation. Wanted to come back as a clam. He told me so, one day when I was fillin' your oil tank. Har-har.*

Shit.

"What's wrong with you?" Oops, I guess I said it out loud.

"Where do you think he's gone?"

"I dunno. Heaven, I guess." Don takes his hands off the wheel for a moment, shrugs. "If there is one, he's there."

"For sure," says Gord. "What do you think?"

"I'm not sure. I think he's in us, you know, genetically, but I think there's something else. Something we can't know about. Like, I mean, *who* he was has to live on. It's up to us now to live that."

"Tall order, Nikki."

"Yeah, but we've got to or…" Shoot, now it's me crying "…or, what's the point?"

Just as I say it, something white flashes in front of the car. Don swerves to avoid it, but can't. A flash of fur rolls up the hood and across and over the windshield. We're riding the shoulder on a precarious slant. "Holy shit!"

"Hang on." Don's struggling to control the truck, slowing. All I hear is the sound of churning gravel roaring in my ears. I wonder briefly if we're going to roll, but we somehow stay upright, pitched forward by the momentum of the careening truck. When at last we stop there is a moment of silence. Don stares ahead, open-mouthed. Gord bows his head and pinches the bridge of his nose, eyes squeezed shut. He's likely seeing — and erasing — what could have happened had the truck pitched end over end, the three of us flung about like rag dolls, the final crush of metal and then flames as the gas tank exploded.

"My God..." says Don and I can't tell whether it's a prayer or a curse. "What the heck was that?"

"A coyote?" I venture.

"A small deer?"

"But it was white."

"And big," says Don. "Really big."

Gord gets out first, and goes to look at the front of the truck. The grille is smashed, the headlights askew and there's some liquid pooling on the ground. The engine smells hot. My brother whistles, long and low, in the darkness. Don joins him and together they poke at the damage, assessing and appraising and muttering to each other.

I start walking away from the truck. I want to see what it is we hit. I hope that it's dead, whatever it is. I hope there is not a wounded animal, wild with pain and shock, in the dark night ahead of me. But how could anything have survived that impact? I walk for what seems to be a long way. The tail lights of the parked truck disappear as I revisit the road we've just traveled. The voices of my brothers fade.

Then I see something white, almost luminous, in the ditch. It's the body of a great white dog. Not a wolf, not an albino mule deer, not a sacred white buffalo, just a dog. A big, dead dog. It's an Alsatian or a Samoyed and it's lying there with its eyes closed as though it's asleep. There seems to be no blood on the body, nothing but masses of white fur. The animal wears no collar, and when I squint into the shadows, I can see the fine tips of the ears and a snout. The dog's mouth is slightly open but there is no breath coming out of it. By the utter silence I know the dog is well and truly dead. I crouch beside it and feel a mighty urge to plunge my hands into the fur, to seek some warmth, and massage the body back to life. I resist by digging my hands deep into the pockets of my jeans. I look at the dog and then straight up to the sky. There is a fingernail moon and the stars are everywhere, blinking back at me in cold splendour. There are thousands of them. Layers and layers of stars, faint and bright, planets and constellations, glinting and glimmering like mica on a black beach and there, weaving and dodging among those stars, is the hushed green ghostly dance of the northern lights.

He will make the face of heaven so fine that all the world will be in love with night.

I hear the rasp of footsteps approaching. The boys' shadows and voices mount the rise in the road. I quickly reach out and touch the white dog before they materialize. The fur is coarse and cold. Nothing lives here anymore.

"What should we do?" Don asks, looking down at the two of us in the ditch.

"Any collar, Nikki?"

"Nope." I rise.

"We'll just leave him then." Gord shrugs. "When's the last time we passed a house?"

"Miles back," said Don. "I looked at the map. I figure we're about ten minutes north of McLennon, just a few minutes outside Peace River. Anyone remember McLennon?"

"They must have had their lights off when we drove by," said Gord, laughing. "Trying to find the owner of this fellow would be like trying to find a needle in a haystack. I'd say we leave him, let nature take its course. I think we can limp into Peace River. We've got to find someone to fix the truck."

"At ten o'clock at night?"

His voice rises a notch. "Got any better ideas, Nikki?"

"I think we should take the dog, too."

"What? Are you nuts?"

"We can't just leave him here, Don. We killed him."

"Oh, for Christ's sake, Nikki. He ran in front of the truck. What are we going to do with a dead dog?"

"'Specially if we end up with a dead truck," chimes in Gord. "Come on, Nikki. Get a grip."

So I go with them, glancing back once at the dog, unmarked and unmoving. I feel a great weight, like someone is squeezing my chest, and it stays with me as the truck, wheezing and weary, navigates the dark lonely highway until it drops off into the last large river valley that cradles the Peace. The town is like a torch and all I know is that it fades the sky and bleaches out my vision of the stars and my father and the accidental death of the white dog. I let the boys deal with the mechanic in the grease monkey suit at the garage we finally find off Main Street. I sit in the cab while they banter and barter and I think about another time in Peace River on one of those countless and interchangeable summer holiday road trips.

When you travel from Yellowknife to Edmonton, the Peace River is an arrival of sorts. It is the first physical land formation that delineates North from South. The border between northern Alberta and the Northwest Territories does too, I suppose, and there was always a sense of jubilation when we passed the great placard that proclaims *I've been North of 60*. Heck, North of 60 we knew. It was our country.

South of 60 was something completely different, something new, a land that held immeasurable appeal. And that great rift in the land, the fissure of the Peace River valley, marked the fact that we were close to the tantalizing promise of the prairies. From a gas station not dissimilar to the one we are now parked in, I was sure I could smell the city. South of Peace River was the beginning of mystery.

It is a small town, of course. Smaller than our own transitory town in the bedrock, but imbued in my child's mind with transformative power. Weren't the houses more interesting here? Wasn't the green girder bridge something else? My brothers and I would thrill at Peace River, the long descent into the town invested with danger. Did we half hope the station wagon would lose control and careen down the switchback highway as we called out to each other *Look at that! Wowee! Holy crow!* from the very back, our noses pressed to the dusty windows?

Whatever it was, the childish abandon and the excitement of arriving at Peace River was enough that Dad used to put us out of the car on the southern banks of the river and tell us to make our own way to the top. We'd delight at the station wagon disappearing up the zigzag hill and, punch-drunk with freedom and fresh air, we would whoop and scramble up the carved-out river bank, a strenuous twenty-minute 250-metre vertical climb that left us red-faced and panting, again ready for the final third of our outward journey. Dad slept up there at the top, forty winks, while Mom sat on the edge of the valley keeping her ears open for the cry of alarm she always anticipated when the competitive spirit seized all five of us at the same time and we'd pull each other backwards, the more quickly to make our own ascent. Dad viewed it as nothing more than a grand scale version of King of the Castle and he'd wake and stretch and take the air himself, grinning ruefully at his gaggle of ragtag children, filthy with the grey-brown clay of the Peace River valley upon them.

This memory is so sweet now that it's night, now that Gord and Don and I are stuck in a greasy garage and Dad's in a box no bigger than the shoeshine kit of our childhood. This memory of Peace River is why, probably for the last time, I will ride this familiar road with my brothers. It's why it is important that we take him home, not by air, but along this dusty gravel road that snakes though the brutal boreal forest that lies ahead.

My brothers' faces appear like dual moons rising through the fogged-up truck windows. They're revved up and crackling with energy, like something base in them has been ignited. Amazing what talk of pistons and carburetors and crankshafts can do to men.

"He's a bloody genius," says Gord, talking over top of me as though I'm not there.

"Who?" I ask.

Don glances at me as if I'm the village idiot. "Chuck."

"Chuck?"

"Yeah, Chuck." He thumbs in the direction of the shop. "Amazing guy. He loves these older models. He's going to have us back on the road in half an hour, with a new rad, grille, the whole shebang."

"He's got a cousin who owns a wrecker's yard, says he'll have the parts here in ten minutes. You don't get that type of personal service in the city, that's for sure. Must be a northern thing."

"We're going to go for a beer while we wait," says Don directly to me. "You might as well come."

"With Chuck?"

"No, while Chuck puts in the new parts. What else you going do, Nikki? Mope about that dog?"

He's right, but I'm pissed off that he said it. I don't know if I can handle listening to my brothers' car-speak in some dive of a draught tavern in Peace River, so I opt out. "I'm going to walk to the bridge. I'll meet you guys back here in half an hour. If Mighty Mechanic has things patched up by then, we can hit the road before midnight, so don't get too comfortable at the bar."

"You think you should be walking around alone so late at night?" Gord asks, sounding genuinely concerned.

"It's Peace River, remember? The gateway to the gateway to the North."

They smirk and wave me off, and I wander down the street in the direction of the river. The air is clearer up here, the stars closer. Above the cliffs on the north side of the river, the northern lights appear faintly. Apparently tourism is a big trade in Yellowknife now that the mines have closed down. Japanese people come on their honeymoons, hundreds of them. They have been told it is extremely fortunate to conceive your first child under the northern lights and so they come to copulate, hoping that the ghostly presence of leaping lights in the sky will make them a perfect child. We were all conceived under those conditions and I don't think any of us are so exceptional. My brothers are slurping beer in some dark roadhouse, my older brother and sister are at home planning a memorial service, and I'm wandering around a strange town wondering where that damn dog came from and, more importantly, where it's gone.

As promised, Chuck has us back on the road shortly after 11:30. He tries to convince us to stay in town — "Nothing to speak of 'tween here and the border" — but after much back and forth between them, we gas up and press on. The truck purrs like a cat after cream as we climb out of the Peace River valley.

The night trip is dark and the miles pass by interminably. My brothers change drivers every hour to stave off boredom and fatigue, so it is a halting, jerky journey down that dark tunnel of road. I offer to drive but they want me for company. My job is to stay awake and talk to the driver while the other one sleeps.

We talk about Dad, playing "Remember the Time" and, mostly, we laugh. *Remember the time we got the foster child? Remember the time Dad brought the Inuit family and they stayed for a week? Remember his famous church potluck chicken and the time Justine sat on the piece of pumpkin pie? Remember the five-day camping trip and how we wore the same clothes every day? Remember Mom freaking out when she saw the pictures? Remember him trying to quit smoking and the sound of him sucking on the empty pipe? Remember Christmas? All the packages of golf tees and pipe cleaners we gave him? It was like each one was the best, the very best possible gift he could receive. Remember?*

And as the early spring sun steals the darkness from the cab of the truck, our words cease. The stars are gone, faded, snuffed out and a phrase from Rob's eulogy creeps back into my sleep-addled mind. *All the world will be in love with night...*

"Let's stop for breakfast," says Gord, waking from his cramped position against the door, hair ridiculously flattened on one side.

"Yeah," says Don. "I'm wiped. I sure could use a coffee."

"I'll drive from Enterprise to the ferry. It's only an hour and some, but first let's stop and get some real food."

"There used to be an Esso with a decent restaurant in Enterprise."

"It's only a couple of klicks. We can pick up a ferry schedule, too."

I'd forgotten about the ferry ride across the Mackenzie. I loved that piece of the journey, the diesel smell, the tug of the current, getting out of the car and watching the mighty river over a mile across, boiling and grey-green, slurping and slopping against the bow of the boat. The anticipation of it after thirteen hours in the truck makes my heart light. We're going to cross the Mackenzie River, that huge arterial flow that leads directly to the Arctic Ocean.

The Mackenzie is a lifeline to isolated communities on the Arctic coast. A barge goes down the river every summer to bring supplies — everything from toilet paper to skidoos — to the remote towns and isolated hamlets at the Mackenzie delta and beyond. The barge loads at the headwaters, Fort Providence, where the river meets Great Slave Lake. That's where we cross. Our town is three hundred kilometres around that lake, on the north arm. That is our destination, and this is our day of arrival. Today, once the frost has burned off the windshield, and we have food in our bellies, we'll get across the great river and traverse the first third of that inland sea, and then we will be home. Then our father, who died in a strange land, will be home, too.

But, it doesn't happen like that. There is a glitch. There are twelve or thirteen rigs lined up like dominoes behind the Esso. The restaurant is abuzz.

"It went out last night."

"Woke up the whole town."

"It's early this year. Global warming."

"Jay's got three rigs on the other side, have to sit empty for up to a month. That'll cost him a pretty penny."

"Bad timing."

"Not putting the boat in until the pack ice clears. Could be up to two weeks before they'll launch. Same thing, year after year. Surely they'll have to start thinking about a bridge soon."

"Cost of produce'll go up, that's for sure. Air freight's expensive. Pity the people on the other side. What they got is what they're left with, that's for sure."

All three of us know, now, what's happened and we hunch over our coffees, despondent and perplexed. What the hell is supposed to happen now? How could we have forgotten about break-up? My brothers are cheered by their eggs, distracted by their food, but I am still edgy and anxious when my French toast arrives with a casual "Here you are, hon" from the waitress.

Hon. It makes me think of my mother at home. I can see the house filled with friends and flowers. Rob probably did the drinks thing last night when the cronies came over, the golfing buddies, the old-timers. He'd be taking Dad's place without even realizing it. The kitchen would be filled with Mom's friends and the talk would be of the shock, of the suddenness of it all, and how easily it could have been one of theirs. The casseroles would be pouring into the house now, it would be awash in food, friends, talk of Dad. Maybe people would be telling stories already, like we did last night. Jeez, I want to be there so badly I can feel it in my body. It's an ache, a longing.

I pick at my food while we formulate a plan.

We'll go to Fort Providence to see for ourselves. If the ice is really out and the ferry not risking the crossing we'll figure it out from there.

"Might as well get our information direct from the source," says Gord. "If we really can't get across, we'll have to work something else out." He's anxious like I am. It must be the box with Dad's ashes that's pulling on our conscience. We promised we'd bring him home. People need to know he's home. We gulp second cups of coffee and pull out of the Esso before the sun is too high in the sky.

Word at the ferry landing is as we suspect. The ice went out last night; the ice road had been closed for two days. There is no way to get across the mile-wide river. A trucker loitering by his rig opens a small crack of hope: "You can drive into Hay River and catch a commercial flight from there," he says, peering into our faces. " I heard they're pretty booked up. Likely as not, you won't get 'cross till Saturday. Cars could be on this side as much as a week, depending on the ice. It's a heavy ice year. Yup, heavy ice." He whistles through a space in his teeth and turns away from our truck to look out at the great pans of ice floating past. "Haven't seen ice like this on the Mackenzie since '72. That was a bad break-up. Nothing moved for six weeks."

"Shit." Don slumps on the steering wheel, smashing his fist against the dash. "Shit. Shit. Shit." He's tired and strung out, but so am I. So is Gord. He's not helping anything. Gord tells him to take it easy and Don tosses him a casual "fuck off."

"Okay, okay. Enough," I say, glaring at both of them in turn, hoping to defuse the tension. "Let's figure out something else. We could try for Hay River airport and tell them, just tell them, about the memorial service and everything. Maybe they'd give us one of those compassionate tickets or something."

"Yeah, they probably would, *if* they had room on the flight."

"Let's call home," says Gord, suddenly decisive. "We can at least let Mom and them know what's happened."

It's the only plan we've got, so Don and I wait in the truck while Gord heads into the Other Side café, a ramshackle log building advertising Coca-Cola and road maps.

"Did I ever tell you about the white-out?" my younger brother asks suddenly, gazing out the window at the streaming river of ice.

"No."

"Oh. Dad and I were coming out in the winter once. I think it was for a Boy Scout jamboree or something because there were a lot of my friends in the car. It was the old blue Rambler. Remember?"

I just nod and my brother talks, his eyes never leaving the river. "The weather was really dirty, snow and blowing snow. It must have been mid-winter. February, I think. I remember I was in the front seat with Dad and you could hardly see a thing. The windshield was frosted over pretty bad, and the whole car was hushed just because it was so scary not knowing what was coming at us. Dad was really concentrating on staying on the road, when we saw the sign for the Mackenzie River ice road. We carried on, out of the trees and onto the river, onto this great stretch of ice."

He pauses, remembering.

"Yeah?"

"Suddenly we couldn't see anything. The white took over. White snowdrifts on either side, white road, white sky, white snow. You couldn't see either shore, so there were no trees. It was like driving in a cloud. Dad couldn't tell where the road was, let alone what side he was supposed to be on, and through the white we could hear these rigs coming at us. That, and the sound of the ice groaning. It was just crazy, not being able to see and hearing these wild noises. Really scary.

"Anyway, Dad couldn't stop for fear of getting rear-ended, so you know what he did? He heaved Alan Dyck's dog, Molly, out the door onto the ice. Remember Molly, Alan's black Lab? Really mellow dog with the grey muzzle? She used to go everywhere with Alan. Anyway, this black dog led us across. It was amazing because Molly was the only thing we could see in all that white, Molly trotting along ahead of us, hugging the snowbank, bringing us across the Mackenzie. Cool, eh?" Don grins over at me "We stopped here, at this place, and Dad bought Molly a whole package of beef jerky." He turns quickly away from me but not before I see there are tears in his eyes. "I'll never forget that, Nikki, that black dog on the ice, leading us across."

His voice trails off into silence and we both look through the scanty spruce on the bank to the river propelling huge pans of ice north to the Arctic Ocean.

Suddenly Gord's back. He's got a smile on, ear to ear. He vaults into the truck, words flying: "They're going to send a plane. One of the cronies has a little propeller number. He's going to land in Hay River around four. They're coming to get us. Rob's set it all up. Hey, you guys, we're going to make it home tonight after all!"

There's no rush anymore. We've only got another hour of driving. Don pulls into a roadside turn-out by the river, cracks his window, puts his head back on the seat and shuts his eyes. I lean into Gord, who's leaning against the passenger window. We ignore the sun casting its blue shadows on the snow, and we sleep.

The plane lands on time. Once again it is the three of us on the tarmac, watching the sky as the little Beechcraft descends, growing larger and larger and finally setting down, shooting past, and circling back to stop in front of us. My brothers hold our luggage. I carry the box that holds Dad.

The box is lighter than I'd expected it to be but it's an awkward mini-coffin shape. For some reason I think it feels warm.

A man gets out of the plane. The propellers are left turning so he ducks low under the wing and comes over to us. I recognize him. It's Mr. Dyer, our neighbour. He wordlessly clasps my brothers' hands and pulls them a little bit towards him. When he comes to me and sees the box in my arms, he pauses and then closes his eyes and puts his arm around me, tight across my shoulders. We follow him to the plane, automatically hunching down against the force of the wind and the whirling blades of the propeller. We climb the little pop-out stairway and, once inside, settle into seats.

There are four on each side and two in the front. It's really compact. Wally Sawchuk, another old friend of my dad's, sticks his head out of the cockpit. He gives us the thumbs-up sign and starts to turn the plane around on the runway. It's noisy inside, so no one can talk. Gord and Don, together on one side of the plane, snap on lapbelts. Mr. Dyer goes forward. I am alone on the other side, next to the window. Dad's box sits next to me, unbuckled. We taxi, the plane shakes like crazy, and then with that weird gut-churning thrust, we are airborne.

The green Chev, sitting in the gloom of long-term parking, looks like a Dinky Toy below. We are steadily climbing. Beside me the sun is low and the clouds are tinged with pink. The ice lake, Great Slave, stretches below us like white hospital sheets. I look for the headwaters of the Mackenzie and the cracking, churning broken ice we saw from the shore, but we are too high. I know that somewhere below, the ice-clogged river flows fast and furious to the sea, but it's difficult to hold that memory in my mind when all I can see is miles and miles of ice. Before the sun is completely extinguished, I see the shadow of our plane, a small dark spot making its way across the forever expanse of the lake.

We are going home. I put my hand on the box next to me and feel its strange warmth creep into my skin. The engine drones. The inside of the aircraft is dark. I can barely make out my brothers across from me. The instrument panel in the front glows green and red. Someone else is, at last, in charge. I imagine my heart inside my chest like a bruised plum. Even my bones are weary and I briefly close my eyes and allow the pure white to spread itself out inside me.

As the plane whines through the night I open my eyes once more to the cool glass and look out to the northern sky. For a brief second I see in the stars the form of a great white dog leaping across the sky. In its wake are the souls of hundreds and hundreds of babies, Japanese babies, but others too, hundreds of babies, winking and rolling and spinning like orbs of dancing light, waiting impatiently to be born.